DEPRAVED

FILTHY DIRTY ROCK STARS

MARGO BOND COLLINS
LONDON KINGSLEY

INTRODUCTION

Hello! Thank you so much for picking up one of our books. We really hope you love it!

We'd hate to part ways once you finish this book, however—so let's keep in touch! We have a great bunch of people in our Readers' Groups that you absolutely shouldn't miss out on. We do exclusive book freebies, online parties, giveaways, sneak previews, and events for this amazing group.

And as a huge thank you for joining, you'll receive free books on us.

Join Here

ABOUT DEPRAVED

IslandFest is a gig to die for...but she might just be the woman they'll all choose to live for.

It's been over a year since Burn Strategy's drummer died in the bus wreck that left the other three band members with a trashed tour schedule, a recording contract they haven't yet been able to complete, and more than one case of raging PTSD.

But now they're back together, planning their comeback show as part of IslandFest.

But the new drummer their manager hired for the week wasn't what any of the guys expected. She's funny, flirtatious, and sexy as hell—and she plays like she's possessed by the ghost of John Bonham himself.

Everyone knows it's a bad idea for anyone in the band to get involved with her.

Much less everyone.

Right?

Rock stars. Girls. Drinks. And one week on an island. What could be better?

Welcome to IslandFest, a seven-day rock and roll experience with dozens of bands from around the world, and over a hundred thousand fans.

In the tropical heat, with gorgeous musicians and stunning beachgoers, things are bound to get sticky.

... in more ways than one.

Depraved is part of the Filthy Dirty Rock Stars shared world collection. It is a stand-alone Reverse Harem Rock Stars Romance, complete with HEA and no romantic cliffhangers.

Please note: this book is a contemporary romance that contains mature content. If such materials offend you, please do not read.

OUR SECRETS

BY BURN STRATEGY

In the darkest corners where shadows crawl,
We come alive when the night begins to fall.
Whispered confessions in a clandestine dance,
A symphony of secrets, a forbidden chance.

Eyes locked in mystery, bodies entwined,
Unveiling desires we've kept confined.
In this realm of temptation, no judgment to find,
Tonight we'll surrender, leave the world behind.

We all have secrets, hidden deep within,
Unleash the flame, let the fire begin.
In this twisted game of seductive deceit,
We'll dance on the edge, our passions discreet.

Underneath the moonlight's sultry embrace,
We embrace the darkness, lost in its grace.
Whispers like silk, trailing down your skin,
Unleashing desires from deep within.

Guitars wail with a fiery desire,
As we ignite this sensual pyre.
Heartbeats racing, the rhythm takes control,
Bodies moving in sync, our hunger unfolds.

We all have secrets, hidden deep within,
Unleash the flame, let the fire begin.
In this twisted game of seductive deceit,
We'll dance on the edge, our passions discreet.

Morning breaks, and reality sets in,
But the memories linger, a forbidden sin.
We'll keep our secrets, locked away tight,
A stolen moment, an electric night.
Eyes still burning, with that secret flame,
We'll carry it with us, never the same.
In the daylight, we'll wear our masks,
But in the shadows, we'll all four bask.

We all have secrets, hidden deep within,
Unleash the flame, let the fire begin.
In this twisted game of seductive deceit,
We'll dance on the edge, our passions discreet.

We all have secrets, we'll never reveal,
A taste of the forbidden, a love we conceal.
In the depths of desire, we find our release,
In the dark of the night, our secrets find peace.

FENDER

The nightmare always starts the same way: the curve of the road in front of us.

The other car coming out of the darkness.

The bus, the screams…

And then the silence.

I bolt upright in bed, heart pounding like a jackhammer in my chest. The sheets cling to me, drenched in sweat, as if they too remember the crash that took our drummer's life.

With each ragged breath, I try to shake off the memory, willing it back into the darkness of my subconscious.

"Damn it," I curse under my breath, glancing at the clock. It's only 4 am. Sleep's not coming back anytime soon. Not for me, not tonight.

I swing my legs over the edge of the bed, feeling the familiar chill of the hardwood floor beneath my feet. Reaching for the bottle of whiskey on the nightstand, my hand hovers above it for a brief moment. I shouldn't, but the temptation is too strong. Uncapping the bottle, I take a swig, wincing as the liquid fire scorches its way down my throat. For now, it helps numb the pain—the ever-present guilt and grief that threatens to consume me.

"Is this what you want?" I mutter bitterly to myself, using my actual birth name like it's some kind of penance. "Drowning your sorrows in a goddamn bottle?"

"Karl" was who I used to be—the one who led the band with confidence and a rebellious spirit that pushed all boundaries. But Fender... Fender is a different beast altogether. The weight of responsibility sits heavy on his shoulders, the crushing need to rebuild what we've lost threatening to break him down.

"Can't go back now," I remind myself, knowing that there's no turning back the clock. I can feel the fear creeping up on me—the fear of losing it all again if I let someone new in, both professionally and personally. But dwelling on it won't bring David, our former drummer, back, and it damn sure won't help the band.

"Time to face the music," I say aloud, a hint of defiance in my voice. I push myself to my feet, ready to conquer the demons that haunt me—one note at a time.

I stumble into the bathroom, my reflection in the mirror a ghostly reminder of what I used to be. Dark circles carve hollows under my eyes, and my cheeks are gaunt from the weight I've lost. I clench my jaw, the muscles flexing.

"Get it together," I growl at my reflection. "For them. For you."

My knuckles turn white as I grip the edge of the sink, taking deep breaths until I regain some semblance of composure. Turning away, I don the armor that is my worn leather jacket, allowing Fender to take control once again.

LATER THAT DAY, WE GATHER IN OUR DINGY REHEARSAL SPACE. The air is thick with tension, the remnants of our shattered dreams scattered across the room like discarded guitar picks.

"We need to figure this out—how to salvage what's left of our careers," I say, forcing a smile onto my face.

"Can we even do that?" asks Vaughn, our bassist, his voice heavy with doubt. "I mean, without a drummer..."

"Of course we can," I snap, maybe too harshly. But I can't stand the idea of giving up, not when music is the only thing that's ever made sense in my life. "We'll find someone new— we have to. This isn't just about us; it's about the fans, too. We owe it to them, and to ourselves."

The others nod, though I can tell they're still reeling from the loss. But I won't let that stop us. It's been almost a year now—and although we're only just now coming out of our grief-stricken depression, it's time to move on.

We need each other now more than ever, and I'll be damned if I let this band fall apart on my watch.

"Okay," I say, clapping my hands together. "Let's go over the schedule and see what we can salvage."

We work well into the night, fueled by a trembling cock- tail of misery and determination. The weight of our shared grief hangs heavy in the air, but we push it aside, focusing on the task at hand. We know that to honor the memory of our lost brother, we'll have to carry on without him—as much as it hurts.

"Karl—" Vaughn hesitates, calling me by my real name for the first time in weeks. "Are we going to be okay?"

"Yeah," I say, though the word feels like a lie on my lips. "We'll make it through this together."

My fingers drum on the table, an echo of my racing thoughts.

"Guys, we need a new direction." I look at each of my bandmates in turn, steeling myself for whatever pushback they might have. "We're not just going to pick up where we left off. We're going to rebrand ourselves, put together a spectacular comeback show."

"Rebrand?" Vaughn's brow furrows. "What do you mean?"

"New image," I say, leaning forward. "Something fresh. We've changed as a band. We've been forced to grow because of what happened. We need our music to reflect that."

"Sounds like a hell of a lot of work," mutters Zach, who plays rhythm guitar, running a hand through his shaggy hair.

"Of course it'll be hard. But it's necessary if we want to stay relevant," I argue. My heart is pounding now, urging me onward. "I'll talk to Ezra"—our manager—"get his input. If we're all in this together, we can make it happen."

"Okay," Vaughn says slowly. "If you think it's what we need, I'm in."

"Me too," chimes in Zach.

"Good." I stand, feeling a spark of hope ignite within me. "Let me call Ezra and set up a meeting."

Later, alone in the apartment, I dial Ezra's number, pacing back and forth as the phone rings.

"Karl! Good to hear from you," Ezra greets me, his voice warm and familiar. "How's the band holding up?"

"Been better, but we're working on it," I say. "Listen, we need your help. We want to rebrand ourselves and stage a spectacular comeback show. We need your guidance on how to best approach this."

"That's a big undertaking," Ezra replies cautiously. "I can't make any promises, but I'll see what I can do. Let's meet tomorrow and discuss it further."

"Thanks. That means a lot," I say, relief washing over me. "We need you now more than ever."

"Of course. I've always believed in you guys. I'll do my best to help you through this," Ezra assures me. "I'll see you tomorrow."

"Sounds good. Thanks again." I hang up the phone, feeling a renewed sense of purpose. The road ahead is going to be tough, but with the support of my bandmates and our manager, we have a fighting chance.

As I lay down in bed that night, my thoughts drift back to the bus wreck, to the loss of David, and to the deep well of grief and guilt that still threatens to consume me. But there's a new emotion mixed in with the pain—a fierce drive to prove to the world, and to myself, that we can come back stronger than ever before.

We owe it to ourselves. And we owe it to David.

Later that evening, I find myself alone in the dimly lit rehearsal space, my fingers hovering over the guitar strings. The room is filled with the ghosts of past jam sessions, and I can almost hear David's laughter echoing off the walls. I take a deep breath and start playing one of our old songs, the notes flowing from my fingertips like water.

As I play, a torrent of emotions surges through me—sorrow for the loss we've experienced, anger at the cruel twist of fate that took him from us, and determination to rise above it all. My fingers fly across the fretboard, faster and more furious than ever before, channeling every ounce of pain and passion into the music. The familiar chords reverberate throughout the room, filling the empty spaces left by his absence.

———

THE NEXT DAY, I MAKE MY WAY TO EZRA'S OFFICE, STEELING myself for the critical conversation we're about to have. As I step inside, I'm greeted by the familiar smell of coffee and vinyl records, a comforting reminder of the countless hours we've spent here discussing the band's future.

"Karl, good to see you," Ezra says, gesturing for me to take a seat. "I've been thinking about your proposal, and I have a few ideas on how we might be able to move forward."

"Great," I say tersely, my jaw clenched in anticipation. "What do you have in mind?"

Ezra leans back in his chair, steepling his fingers as he considers his words. "Well, first things first, we need to finish recording that album."

At the mention of the unfinished album, something inside me snaps. A tidal wave of memories comes crashing down, overwhelming me with guilt and grief. I see flashes of the bus wreck, the twisted metal, and the lifeless body of our drummer. My hands tremble, and my breaths come in short, ragged gasps.

"Hey, you okay?" Ezra asks, concern etching lines across his face.

"Sorry," I mumble, struggling to regain control of myself. "I just... I need a moment." Without waiting for a response, I push back from the table and head outside, gasping for air as if I've been submerged underwater.

Leaning against the cold brick wall of the building, I struggle to process the onslaught of emotions that have blindsided me. It's been months since the accident, but the pain still feels as raw and fresh as it did on that terrible day. How can I possibly lead the band through this storm when I'm barely keeping my own head above water?

As I stand there, shivering in the chilly Denver air, I know that I can't keep running from my demons. If we're going to survive this, I need to confront the darkness within me and find a way to channel that pain into something positive.

Taking a deep breath, I square my shoulders and reenter the office, determination burning like a fire in my chest. "Let's do this. Let's finish what we started."

"Good man," Ezra replies, nodding solemnly. "We'll get through this together."

For the first time in what feels like an eternity, I allow myself to believe that maybe, just maybe, things are going to be all right.

Back at my apartment, I toss my keys onto the counter and glance around the dimly lit room. The shadows seem to grow darker, reminding me of the haunting memories that have plagued me since the accident.

It's now or never, I think, clenching my fists as I brace myself for the emotional maelstrom that's been lurking beneath the surface.

"Okay," I mutter under my breath, "time to face the music."

Inhaling deeply, I allow the memories to wash over me, forcing myself to confront the guilt and grief head-on. Images of the twisted wreckage and broken drumsticks dance before my eyes, each one more vivid than the last.

"Damn it," I growl, slamming my fist into the wall. The pain in my knuckles barely registers, overshadowed by the overwhelming weight of my emotions. "Why did this happen? Why him?"

"Karl?" a tentative voice calls out from behind me. Startled, I turn to see Zach standing in the doorway, his usually confident demeanor replaced by a look of concern. "Dude, you okay?"

"Zach," I sigh, rubbing my temples. "What are you doing here?"

"Thought I'd check on you after the meeting with Ezra. You seem pretty shaken up," he replies hesitantly, taking a step toward me.

"Thanks, man," I say, attempting to muster a weak smile. "But I'm fine. Just...processing everything, y'know?"

"Look," Zach begins, his voice gentle yet firm. "We've all been through hell these past few months, and we're all hurting. We need to stick together, though."

I stare at him for a moment, my heart pounding in my chest as I consider the truth in his words. It's been so long since I've allowed myself to be vulnerable, to expose my raw emotions to anyone else. But deep down, I know that Zach is right; if we're going to move forward, we need to lean on each other for support.

"All right," I concede, swallowing the lump in my throat. "I...I've been struggling ever since the accident. The nightmares, the flashbacks...it's like I can't escape it."

"Hey, man," Zach says softly, placing a comforting hand on my shoulder. "It's okay. We're here for you, and we'll help you through this."

"I just don't want to let you guys down."

"You're not letting us down," he insists. "We're a family, and families stick together."

His words resonate deep within me.

We will rise from the ashes and make our comeback, I tell myself.

And maybe, just maybe, we'll find some healing along the way.

2

ZACH

The sun is barely peeking through the blinds when I awake with a start. My heart races as I try to shake off the remnants of yet another restless night, plagued by the anxieties that seem impossible to escape these days. I know I can't spend another day drowning in my thoughts. The band needs me, and I have to find a way to ground myself.

Rolling out of bed, I make my way to the small corner of my apartment where I practice yoga each morning. The familiar ritual brings solace amid the chaos, reminding me of the strength within me. As I move through each pose, I focus on my breath, inhaling deeply and exhaling slowly. The tension in my muscles begins to dissipate, replaced by a sense of peace and clarity that prepares me to face whatever challenges lay ahead.

"Think positive," I whisper to myself, forcing a smile as I roll up my yoga mat. "Today's a new day."

It's a weird ritual, one that I started as physical therapy

after my leg was broken in the bus crash. My grief counselor suggested I keep it up once my leg was better—and it's helping me get over David's death. Besides, it beats the fuck out of burying my pain in drugs and alcohol.

By the time I arrive at our rehearsal space, Vaughn and Fender are already there, tuning their instruments.

"Morning," Vaughn greets me, weariness threading through his voice.

"Hey, guys," I reply, mustering as much enthusiasm as I can. "What's on the agenda for today?"

Fender sighs, running a hand through his dark hair. "We need to talk about finding a new drummer."

The words hang in the air like an unwelcome guest, and I can see the weight of it settling on each of us. Our hearts ache for our lost friend, but we can't let our grief consume us if we want the band to survive.

"Look, guys," I say hesitantly, breaking the silence. "I know this is hard for all of us, but we need to keep moving forward. Let's try to focus on what we can do right now."

Fender nods. "Exactly. We can't let this hold us back any longer."

"Maybe we could just...jam for a bit?" Vaughn suggests quietly. "See how it feels without making any decisions yet?"

"Sounds good to me." I pick up my guitar and settle into the familiar rhythm that has always brought us together.

As we play, each chord strikes a bittersweet note. The vibrations of my guitar strings pulse through my body, resonating deep within my chest as I strum the familiar chords. Fender's powerful lead guitar melds with mine, while Vaughn's bass adds depth and richness to our sound. For a moment, it's as if time stands still, and we are all transported back to a happier time in our lives.

"Feels good, doesn't it?" I murmur as I glance at Fender, who is fully immersed in the music, his fingers dancing effortlessly across the fretboard. Our eyes lock for a moment, and I see in his piercing blue gaze a reflection of my own determination to make our comeback a reality. Music has always been our sanctuary.

It will be again.

"Better than you know," Fender replies, a smile tugging at the corner of his mouth.

As we continue playing, I feel the unspoken under-standing between us—the shared drive that will keep us moving forward.

As the song ends, I stare down at my guitar. The strings vibrate softly under my fingers, a faint echo of the music we've just played. But as the last notes fade away, a knot of anxiety tightens in my chest.

"Hey, you okay?" Fender asks, his voice cutting through my thoughts.

I hesitate, torn between the desire to share my fears and the instinct to keep them locked inside. "Yeah, I'm fine," I reply, trying to sound convincing. But the moment our eyes meet, I know he doesn't buy it.

"I know that look. Something's bothering you."

Taking a deep breath, I decide to take the risk and open up to him. "I don't know, man," I admit, my voice shaking slightly. "Sometimes I just worry that I'm not good enough, you know? That I might let you guys down."

Fender's expression softens, and he reaches out to place a hand on my shoulder. "Hey, listen to me," he says firmly. "You are an incredible musician and an even better friend. You've always been there for us, holding this band together when everything seems like it's falling apart. We wouldn't be here without you."

His words bring a sense of relief, and I feel the weight of my anxiety begin to lift. "Thanks," I mumble, feeling a smile tug at the corners of my mouth. "I needed to hear that."

"Anytime, man," he replies with a grin, giving my shoulder a squeeze before turning to the rest of the band. "Hey, why don't we all grab some dinner together? My treat."

"Sounds great," Vaughn agrees, his eyes lighting up at the prospect of food. "I'm starving."

"You're always starving, dude," Fender says.

"Actually," I interject, a sudden burst of confidence surging through me. "Why don't I cook for us tonight?"

"Really?" Fender raises an eyebrow in surprise but quickly smiles. "Okay, chef Zach. We're all yours."

I shift gears into a more practical mindset. "Also, I think it's time for me to take on the responsibility of coordinating our schedule—rehearsals, meetings, the works. We need to stay organized and focused if we're going to pull this off."

"Sounds good to me," Vaughn chimes in, nodding in agreement. "You've always had a knack for keeping us on track."

"Thanks," I say. My ability to stay organized and maintain harmony within the group has always been one of my strengths.

As I pull out my phone to begin planning our schedule, I can't help but marvel at the resilience of our bond. Through the highs and lows, Burn Strategy has remained unbreakable.

I look up from my phone, meeting Fender's gaze once more. "We've got this. Let's bring our music back to life."

"Damn right," Fender agrees, his eyes blazing with renewed determination.

With our shared resolve solidified, we plunge headfirst into planning our comeback, each of us ready to face whatever the future holds.

AT MY APARTMENT LATER, THE SOUNDS OF LAUGHTER AND camaraderie fill the air.

With practiced ease, I chop vegetables and sear tender cuts of meat, the aroma of spices and herbs mingling with the comfortable hum of conversation. The meal comes together beautifully, and as we sit down to eat, I feel a surge of pride at the sight of their eager faces.

"Wow, this is amazing," Vaughn declares after taking his first bite, his eyes widening in delight.

"Seriously," Fender agrees, nodding appreciatively. "You've outdone yourself."

"Thanks," I reply. "I just wanted to do something for all of us."

Like we used to.

The words hang unspoken in the air—but we all carefully ignore them.

As we eat and share stories from our past, the band's bond seems to begin to reassert itself.

The laughter and conversation eventually fade, as the remnants of our meal lie scattered across the table. I notice Vaughn slip away to the living room, an unreadable expression on his face. With a quick glance at Fender, I decide to follow him.

"Hey," I say softly, sitting down beside him on the couch. The setting sun casts long shadows through the window, bathing the room in a warm, golden light.

"Hey," he replies, his gaze fixed on the fading colors of the sky. "I was just thinking."

"About what?"

"How much we've all been through together, and how far we still have to go." He sighs, running a hand through his sandy brown hair. "It's a lot to carry, you know?"

"Tell me about it," I agree, wrapping my arms around my

knees. "Sometimes it feels like we're on this never-ending roller coaster, and I'm just trying to hold on for dear life."

Vaughn nods, turning to look at me. His moss-green eyes seem to see straight into my soul. "You talked to Fender earlier, didn't you?"

I hesitate, caught off-guard by his perceptiveness. "Yeah," I admit. "I guess I just needed someone to talk to. To remind me that I'm not alone in this."

"You're not," he assures me. "We all have our struggles."

"I know you've got a lot weighing on you too," I say, recalling the emotional scars left by the bus wreck and the PTSD that haunts him.

He looks away for a moment, his jaw clenched. "Yeah," he says, his voice strained. "But that doesn't mean I can't be there for the rest of you."

"We're stronger together than we are apart—promise I'll do my best to remember that," I say.

He nods. "Let's get back to the others. We've got a lot of work ahead of us if we're gonna make this comeback a reality."

Shit, isn't that the truth, I think as I follow him back into the kitchen.

3

VAUGHN

The worn leather couch creaks as I lean forward, my fingers tapping rhythmically against the armrest. Zach sits nearby, strumming idly on his guitar, while Fender paces the length of the room, his boots thudding against the floorboards. The air is thick with anticipation, a tangible tension that hangs over us like a storm cloud waiting to burst.

Ezra bursts into the room, clutching a steaming cup of coffee. His eyes gleam with excitement, the look he always gets when he's got good news. "I've got something big for you."

"Spit it out, Ez," Fender growls, stopping his pacing and folding his arms across his chest. He always was impatient when it came to band matters, but I can't say I blame him this time. My heart races in my chest, echoing the pounding beat of an invisible drum.

"IslandFest," Ezra announces triumphantly, setting his coffee down on the table and leaning against the back of a chair. "You guys have been given an opportunity to perform there. This could be exactly what Burn Strategy needs to get back on track."

My breath catches in my throat at the mention of the prestigious rock festival. Images of roaring crowds flash through my mind, a taste of the fame and success we once came so close to capturing—and now crave more than ever.

But there's also an undercurrent of fear and uncertainty running through the room; after all, we're not the same band we were before everything fell apart.

"Are you serious?" Zach asks, his dark brown eyes widening with a mixture of disbelief and hope. His laid-back demeanor fades for a moment, replaced by the passion that has always driven his love for music.

"Dead serious," Ezra replies, grinning from ear to ear. "I know it's last minute, but this is a chance you can't pass up. You guys need to bring your A-game."

"Damn right we will," Fender says with a fierce determination, his blue eyes blazing.

As the band erupts into excited chatter and impromptu planning, I remain silent, taking it all in. IslandFest could be the turning point for us—the moment when our luck finally changes, when our dreams of making a comeback start to become reality.

But the weight of that potential success rests heavily on my shoulders.

There's so much at stake here, and we can't afford to make any mistakes.

"Vaughn?" Fender's voice cuts through my thoughts, and I realize he's been trying to get my attention. "What do you think?"

"IslandFest is huge," I say slowly, choosing my words carefully. "It's an incredible opportunity—we have to give it everything we've got." My gaze locks onto Fender's, silently promising him that I'll fight tooth and nail to make sure Burn Strategy rises from the ashes.

"Then let's do it," he replies.

The room buzzes with renewed energy as we throw ourselves into planning for IslandFest.

We may be battered and bruised, but we're not broken— not by a long shot. This is our chance to prove ourselves, to show the world what Burn Strategy is truly made of.

And I'll be damned if we don't seize it with both hands.

I envision the possibilities this opportunity presents. I can almost taste the electric energy of the crowd, feel the vibration of the stage beneath my feet. This could be it—the breakthrough Burn Strategy has been yearning for. The chance to shed the weight of the past and rise from the ashes like a phoenix reborn.

"All right," I say, taking charge of the situation, "we need to create a detailed timeline for our preparations. This is our shot, and we have to make the most of it." My voice is steady, and I can see the fire in my bandmates' eyes as they nod in agreement.

"First things first," Zach chimes in, his fingers tapping a rhythm on the table. "We need to fine-tune our setlist. Make sure it's tight and showcases our best work."

"Agreed," Fender adds, leaning back in his chair. "We also need to get our equipment checked and sorted. No room for technical issues at IslandFest."

"Right," I say, mentally adding these tasks to the growing list in my mind. "We'll need to coordinate with Ezra for any promotional materials and travel arrangements too."

"Absolutely," Ezra confirms, already typing away on his phone. "I'll start working on that right away."

"Don't forget rehearsals," I continue, my mind racing to cover every detail. "Daily practice sessions and perfecting our stage presence."

"Done," says Zach, and Fender nods in agreement, their determination matching my own.

As we discuss our plan, my thoughts stray to my own struggles. The lingering shadows of PTSD claw at the edges of my consciousness, threatening to undermine my focus.

But I can't let that happen. For the sake of the band, for the sake of our dreams, I have to push through the pain and be the anchor they need me to be.

"Vaughn," Ezra's voice pulls me back to the present. "Do you think you can handle all of this?"

I meet his gaze with a steely resolve. "I can, and I will," I assure him. "We've come too far to let anything stand in our way."

"Then let's make it happen," Fender declares, and we dive back into planning our triumphant return to the stage.

We'll conquer IslandFest and show the world that Burn Strategy is a force to be reckoned with. We'll forge connections and create memories that will last a lifetime—not just for us, but for our fans as well.

"Before we wrap up," Ezra interjects, his voice taking on a serious tone, "there's one more thing. You guys need a new drummer, and we only have a week to find one if you're gonna have enough practice time before the festival.."

My heart skips a beat at the reminder of our missing piece. A week is not enough time to find someone who can seamlessly fit in with us, but failure isn't an option.

"Actually, I may have someone in mind," Ezra continues. "I'll arrange for a meeting tomorrow."

"Thanks," Fender says. And with that, our meeting comes to an end, and we go our separate ways.

Stepping into my apartment less than half an hour later, I'm greeted by the familiar scent of old vinyl records and guitar polish.

My sanctuary.

I set my laptop down on the coffee table, sitting in front of it to search for information about IslandFest.

This festival has been a turning point for many careers, and it could be ours too.

The flicker of hope inside me grows, fueled by the stories I'm reading of success and triumph, but it's tinged with anxiety.

Our band needs to be whole again, and finding the right drummer is crucial. The pressure to make this work is immense.

But I won't let it crush me.

As night falls, I continue researching, each page revealing another facet of the festival that could shape our destiny.

My fingers hover over the keyboard, my pulse quickening as I click through the pages. Images of past IslandFest performances flash before me, along with videos of electrifying sets, fans singing along to lyrics that have become anthems, and artists who've made history on that stage.

My dream of Burn Strategy standing among those legends grows more vivid with each passing moment.

"Vaughn, you're seriously missing out!" Zach's voice breaks through my reverie as he sends a video call request. I accept it, and his grinning face fills my screen. "Check this out! Fender found some old concert footage from our last tour. It's amazing!"

"Show me," I say, my heart swelling with nostalgia as I watch our younger selves performing.

"Imagine us up there again, man," Fender chimes in from off-screen, his voice laden with excitement. "IslandFest could be the start of something huge for us."

I smile at their enthusiasm, knowing that we all share the same burning hope for our future. But as the conversation turns to finding a new drummer, my heart twists.

"Replacing David won't be easy," I say, my throat tightening around the words.

"Hey, no one's ever going to replace David," Zach's reassuring tone softens the blow. "But we have to move forward. Ezra says he has someone in mind, right? Let's give him a chance."

"Zach's right," Fender adds. "We owe it to Dave not to let this opportunity slip through our fingers."

I nod, swallowing the lump in my throat. They're right—we can't let our past hold us back. We have to embrace this chance and make the most of it, for everyone who's ever believed in us.

"Let's do this," I say. "Let's get ready to rock IslandFest."

As the call ends, I stare at the screen, my thoughts racing. The stage lights, the pounding bass, the rhythm of the drums—all of it is within our reach once more.

But we have to find that missing piece, the drummer who will complete our sound and help us rise to new heights.

My fingers tap restlessly on the table, echoing the beat of my heart as I grapple with the mix of emotions coursing through me. It's a strange blend of excitement and fear, of longing for the past while reaching for the future.

"Vaughn Michaels," I whisper to myself, "you've got this."

Finally, I close my laptop, swearing to myself that nothing will stand in our way—not even the race against time to find the perfect drummer.

We'll show the world that Burn Strategy is back and stronger than ever before.

4

DALLAS

The door to the band's rehearsal studio—such as it is —swings open with a loud creak, and I stride in like I own the place. The mischievous smile on my lips doesn't waver, even as I note the surprised expressions on the faces of the three men who make up the would-be rock-and-roll dream team.

"Didn't expect a woman, huh?" I toss my blonde hair over my shoulder, amused. Their shock hits me with the force of a punch, and I enjoy their moment of disorientation. It's not every day you get to shake up the status quo.

"Uh, no, we didn't," Fender admits, running a hand through his tousled dark hair, clearly trying to regroup. "But hey, talent is talent, right?"

"Damn straight." I nod, reveling in the way their eyes follow me as I saunter across the room. They're undoubtedly sizing me up, wondering if I have what it takes to fill the vacant spot behind their drum kit.

As far as first impressions go, I'd say I've already made a memorable one.

"Nice setup you got here," I remark, letting my gaze roam over the assortment of instruments and gear that clutter the space. There's an air of chaos about the room, but beneath it lies the unmistakable pulse of creativity.

This is where the magic happens, and I'm eager to be a part of it.

"Thanks," Zach says, flashing me a grin that highlights the dimples in his cheeks. "We've been working hard to find our sound, but we've been missing that... special something."

"Maybe I can help with that," I say coyly, my fingers itching to make contact with the drumsticks tucked away in my bag.

Vaughn, the quietest of the trio, finally speaks up. "We're definitely curious to see what you can do."

"Curious" doesn't even begin to cover it. The weight of their expectations bears down on me, the hope that maybe— just maybe—I'll be the missing piece they've been searching for. But instead of succumbing to the pressure, I allow it to fuel me.

I've never been one to shy away from a challenge.

"Get ready for a wild ride, boys," I say with a wink, letting my smile morph into something more wicked. "Introductions first," I declare, striding forward with purpose. "I'm Dallas Graham, your new drummer—at least for today." I extend my hand to Fender, who takes it hesitantly, still processing the fact that I'm a woman.

"Karl Finnegan," he says, his grip firm and confident. There's an air of guarded intensity about him, but beneath it, I can sense his passion for music. "But everyone calls me Fender."

I already know their names, of course—I've been

watching videos of their old performances online for days now—but they don't need to know that.

"Nice to meet you," I say, my eyes meeting his briefly before turning to Zach.

"Zach Hayashi," he introduces himself with an easy smile, his dark brown eyes warm and inviting. There's something genuine and authentic about him that I find instantly endearing.

"Last but not least," I say, extending my hand to Vaughn. His dark green eyes seem to hold a quiet strength, and I can tell there's more to him than meets the eye. "And you must be Vaughn Michaels."

"Guilty as charged," he replies, shaking my hand with a reserved nod.

"Let's get this show on the road!" I exclaim, rubbing my hands together eagerly. The anticipation thrums through my veins like electricity, and I can't wait any longer.

Fender nods, his fingers already itching to strum his guitar. "We'll start with 'Rising Storm.' It's one of our heavier tracks; let's see how you handle it."

"Bring it on." I grab my drumsticks and settling in behind the kit. As the opening chords ring out, I take a deep breath and dive into the rhythm, my heart pounding in time with the beat.

My sticks fly across the drums, lightning-fast and precise. The sound reverberates through the studio, a powerful force that fills every corner of the room. I can feel the energy building, an electricity that crackles and sparks between us.

"Damn," Fender mutters under his breath as he watches me in awe. "She's good."

"More than good," Zach agrees, his eyes locked on my hands as they dance across the drumheads. "She's amazing."

I revel in their reactions, but I don't let it distract me. Instead, I focus on the music, letting it wash over me, consume me. My instincts take over, guiding me as I weave intricate patterns into the rhythm, effortlessly matching the intensity of the band's performance.

Vaughn's bass thumps through the floor and into my bones while Fender's guitar wails, its mournful cry weaving around Zach's melodic strumming. The music thrums through every fiber of my being, an indescribable connection that makes my heart soar.

As the song reaches its climax, I give it my all, pushing myself to new heights. Sweat beads on my forehead, stinging my eyes, but I barely notice. The world narrows down to the beat, the pulse, the rhythm that drives us forward.

And then, as suddenly as it began, the song ends. Silence crashes down around us, leaving me breathless and exhilarated. My hands tremble slightly from the adrenaline still coursing through my veins, and I grin at my temporary bandmates.

"Wow," Fender says, visibly impressed. "That was... incredible."

"Thanks," I say, panting slightly. "You guys are pretty amazing too."

"Let's keep this momentum going," Vaughn suggests. "We've got more songs to get through."

"Sounds like a plan," I agree, adjusting my grip on my sticks. "Let's rock this joint."

As we dive into the next song, I know with absolute certainty that I've found something special here. A connection that goes beyond mere words, beyond simple friendship or camaraderie. It's a bond forged in music, in passion.

And I'll do whatever it takes to hold onto it.

Feeling the heat of the lights above and the pulsating energy of the band surrounding me, I let my instincts take over as I add my own flair to the songs. I let my sticks dance across the drum kit like a whirling dervish, infusing unexpected rhythms and creative fills into the music. Each beat breathes new life into the band's sound, and I can feel the excitement radiating from Fender, Zach, and Vaughn.

My versatility and musical intuition shine through, and I seamlessly integrate myself into the music—not just playing alongside them but becoming an essential part of the band's heartbeat. It feels as if I've been playing with these guys for years. Our connection is undeniable.

"Let's take five," Fender announces, wiping the sweat from his brow. The band members disperse, grabbing water bottles and towels. I hop off my drum stool, adrenaline still surging through my veins.

"Damn," Zach says, flashing me a heart-stopping smile. "You've got some serious skills."

"Thanks," I say, taking a swig of water. "You guys make it easy to play along."

"Easy? With that tempo?" Vaughn chuckles, shaking his head in disbelief. "I think you're giving us too much credit."

"Ah, come on now," I tease, grinning at them. "A little self-love never hurt anyone."

"Is that your motto?" Fender smirks, raising an eyebrow. "Because we could all use a dose of your confidence."

"Maybe it's contagious," I suggest playfully, winking at him. His cheeks redden slightly, and I can tell he's trying to suppress a smile. The flirtatious atmosphere is electric, and I find myself basking in the attention of these three gorgeous, talented men.

"Speaking of confidence," Zach says, attempting to regain his composure. "I've never seen someone so in tune with their instrument. It's like you and those drums are one."

"Music is my escape," I confess. "When I'm playing, every-thing else just fades away."

"Couldn't have said it better myself," Vaughn agrees, nodding solemnly.

"Break's over," Fender announces suddenly, clapping his hands together. "Let's get back to work."

As we return to our respective instruments, an over-whelming sense of belonging slams through me.

These guys—this band—they've ignited something inside me.

This is where I belong.

The energy in the room zings through me as I continue to play, my drumsticks dancing across the skins with a newfound confidence. I watch Fender, Zach, and Vaughn's expressions shift from shock to awe as our instruments meld together, forming a beautiful cacophony of sound.

"Guys, hold up for a sec," I call out, bringing my drumsticks to a sudden halt. They glance at me curiously, their fingers stilling on their respective instruments. "I have an idea for that chorus—what if we add a syncopated rhythm here? It might give it some extra punch."

Fender furrows his brow, considering my suggestion. "Show us what you mean," he says, nodding toward my drum kit.

With a grin, I launch into the new rhythm, tapping my foot on the bass pedal and hitting the snare in rapid succession. The band members watch intently, their heads nodding along with the beat. When I finish, I look up to gauge their reactions.

"Damn," Zach breathes, his eyes wide. "That's... that's amazing."

"Seriously," Vaughn agrees, his fingers already itching to join in. "Let's try it all together."

We dive back into the song, incorporating my suggested rhythm change, and the difference is immediate. The chorus feels tighter, more powerful, and the energy in the room surges even higher. Our creative synergy is undeniable, and pride swells within me.

"That's a wrap!" Fender announces after we finish another run-through of the song. We're all slightly breathless, sweat dripping down our faces, but the satisfaction of a successful rehearsal is evident on each of our faces.

"Great job, everyone," I praise, wiping my brow with the back of my hand. "It was an honor to play with you guys."

"Likewise," Zach says, grinning. "You're a force to be reckoned with."

"Hey, can I talk to you for a minute?" Fender asks, gesturing for me to follow him into the small office space.

"Sure," I say, my heart skipping a beat. What could he want to talk about?

Once we're alone, Fender leans against the edge of a cluttered desk, his blue eyes searching mine intently. "Dallas... your talent is undeniable. You've brought something special to our sound that we didn't even realize was missing."

I swallow, feeling a blush creep up my cheeks. "Thank you. That means a lot, coming from you."

"Tell me about your experience and your musical influences. And more importantly, how'd you feel about joining the band permanently?"

"Permanently?" I repeat, the word echoing in my head like a dream.

This is exactly what I've been craving: a chance to be part of something greater. "My influences are all over the place—everything from classic rock to jazz. But as for joining to band..." I hesitate, my fear of commitment briefly bub the surface. , and I

But then I look back at Fender's earnest exr know I can't pass up this opportunity. ure. "More

"I'd love to," I say finally, my voice st than anything."

FENDER

At rehearsal the next day, the dim lighting within the rehearsal studio casts shadows over Dallas's face, her golden hair framing her features and catching the light in a halo around her head. Her sapphire-blue eyes sparkle with mischief as she sits behind the drums, her tiny but surprisingly strong frame commanding the instrument with ease. I stare as her drumsticks fly through the air, creating an infectious rhythm that pulses through my veins.

"Let's take it from the top!" I call out, gripping the neck of guitar tightly, my fingers itching to play. As I strum the waords, my eyes remain locked on Dallas's movements, her breathe life into our music.

sure k he shouts above the noise, grinning widely, "you comebac to pick 'em! This is gonna be one hell of a I chuc

. trying to mask the uneasiness that

gnaws at the pit of my stomach. It's true—her exceptional drumming has injected new life into our sound, and there's no denying that Dallas is exactly what we needed to reignite our passion for music.

I notice the way she beams with pride, her eyes lighting up with excitement. It's in this moment that I realize just how much of a risk I've taken, and as I watch her, a pang of regret for inviting her into our world punches me in the stomach.

I'm deeply attracted to her, and it scares the shit out of me.

"Get your head in the game, Fender!" Zach shouts at me, snapping me out of my thoughts. I force myself to focus on my guitar playing and singing, but my mind keeps drifting back to the decision I've made.

As we continue rehearsing, I can't shake the growing concern that's plaguing me. The band needed harmony and unity, but now I can't help questioning whether adding Dallas to the mix will bring us closer together or create further complexity.

I try to ignore the magnetic pull she exerts on me, knowing all too well that it could jeopardize everything we've worked so hard for.

"Great job, guys!" Dallas exclaims as the song comes to an end.

"All right," I say, putting my guitar down and wiping the sweat from my forehead. "Let's take a break."

As I step outside for some fresh air, I find myself cornered by my own thoughts, unable to escape the weight of the decision I've made. I know I should be celebrating our newfound potential, yet all I can think about is whether I've set us on a path of harmony or a collision course with disaster.

"Hey," Vaughn says, stepping outside behind me and clapping me on the back. "You okay, man?"

I force a smile, attempting to hide my inner turmoil. "Yeah, I'm good," I lie. "Just...thinking."

"About what?"

"Nothing important," I say, trying to shrug it off. But deep down, I know that the consequences of my choices are anything but insignificant.

And back inside a few minutes later as I watch Dallas laughing with Zach, her flirtatious nature stirring something within me, I worry about the delicate balance we've tried so hard to maintain—and whether I've unwittingly tipped the scales toward chaos.

The scent of sweat and sound equipment fills the air as I lean against the wall, watching Dallas take her place behind the drum kit. An electric energy courses through me as she tucks a loose strand of blonde hair behind her ear and flashes me a mischievous grin.

"Ready for round two?" she asks, twirling her drumsticks with practiced ease.

"Bring it on," I say, feeling my pulse quicken at her flirtatious tone, even as a single word runs through my mind over and over.

Fuck, fuck, fuck.

As we launch into another song, I find myself captivated by Dallas's drumming. The passion in her movements is intoxicating—the way her arms swing gracefully, striking the drums with an intensity that sends shivers down my spine.

Despite my reservations, I'm secretly in awe of her skill, the raw talent she brings to our music.

"Man, she's incredible," Zach whispers, echoing my thoughts as he watches from beside me. "We've never had this kind of energy before."

I nod, unable to tear my eyes away from the sight before me.

"Hey Fender," Dallas calls out during a brief pause in the music, her blue eyes sparkling with mischief. "You look like you're lost in thought over there. Care to share?"

"Uh, nothing important," I stammer, caught off guard by her directness. "Just focusing on the music."

"Right." She smirks, clearly not buying my excuse. "Well, just try to keep up, okay?"

"Always," I shoot back, engaging in the playful banter that seems to come naturally between us. As we dive into the next song, I wonder whether it's worth the risk.

In between songs, I take the opportunity to observe Dallas more closely. I watch her hands deftly move across the drum kit, her fingers gripping the sticks with unwavering precision. The way she loses herself in the music, her eyes closed as she sways to the rhythm, sends a shiver down my spine.

Focus, I chide myself silently, shaking off the thoughts that threaten to consume me. *You've got work to do.*

As we finish up rehearsal, I can't deny the allure of Dallas's drumming or the passion she brings to our music. And though I have mixed emotions, I know I need to find a way to navigate these complexities if we're to have any hope of making a successful comeback.

"Great session, guys," Dallas says, wiping away a bead of sweat from her brow. Her smile is infectious, and I find myself grinning back, despite the storm of emotions brewing inside me.

"Thanks," I say, knowing that only time will tell if I've made the right decision.

For now, I'll embrace the undeniable energy that she brings to our band.

"Anybody up for drinks?" Dallas asks—and we all three jump at the chance to spend more time with her.

Fuck.

The sounds of laughter fill the small, dimly lit bar we choose for our post-rehearsal gathering. The atmosphere is electric, charged with the newfound energy Dallas has brought to the band. I watch her from across the room, her blonde hair catching the warm glow of the hanging lights as she engages in animated conversation with Vaughn and Zach.

"Hey Fender, you want another drink?" Vaughn calls out.

"Sure," I say, though my mind remains preoccupied. I notice the way Vaughn's gaze lingers on Dallas, the way he leans in just a little too close as they talk. And it's not just him—Zach is equally captivated by her presence, his dark brown eyes filled with curiosity and something deeper.

"Here you go," Vaughn says, handing me a fresh beer. "Cheers to us and our new drummer!"

"Cheers," I echo, forcing a smile as we clink our glasses together. My chest tightens with conflicting emotions.

"Isn't she awesome?" Zach chimes in, his voice tinged with excitement. "I mean, I'm really impressed by her drumming skills."

"Definitely," I agree, my throat feeling dry as I take a swig of my beer. I can't shake the nagging feeling that their growing fascination with Dallas could test their loyalty to each other and to the band.

I can't afford to let things spiral out of control.

"Hey guys," Dallas says, approaching us with a playful grin on her face. "What are you whispering about over here?"

"Nothing much," I say, attempting to sound casual. "Just discussing how great you were during rehearsal."

"Aw, thanks," she replies, her eyes sparkling. "I'm really glad to be a part of this band."

"Us too," Vaughn says, his voice laced with sincerity.

For a moment, we all fall silent, the weight of our unspoken desires settling heavily in the air between us. I can sense the undercurrent of temptation tugging at each of us, threatening to unravel the tight-knit bond we've worked so hard to maintain.

I force a smile as I raise my bottle in a toast. "To new beginnings and the future of our band."

"Cheers!" they all echo, clinking their drinks together. And though I join in their laughter and camaraderie, I wonder if we're truly prepared for the journey ahead—or if the undeniable allure of Dallas will ultimately prove too much for our fragile unity to withstand.

A FEW HOURS LATER, THE SUN SETS BEHIND THE DENVER skyline, casting shadows that creep across the walls of my apartment. I lean against the cool glass of the windowpane.

"Damn it," I mutter under my breath as I confront my own insecurities. My attraction to her is undeniable, but can I resist the temptation she represents?

And what would indulging in that desire mean for our unity and our comeback?

I know I need to talk to the others, to gauge their feelings and ensure we're all on the same page. With a determined sigh, I reach for my phone and send a message to Vaughn and Zach, asking them to meet me back at our rehearsal space in an hour.

"Thanks for coming, guys," I say as they enter the room, pouring whiskey into glasses all around.

"Of course," Zach replies, his dark eyes searching mine. "What's going on?"

"Look, I'm just gonna lay it out there," I admit, taking a

deep breath. "I'm attracted to Dallas. But I don't want anything, any kind of personal entanglement, to jeopardize what we've built together."

Vaughn clenches his jaw, nodding slowly. "I feel the same way. She's incredible, but the last thing I want is for us to lose focus or turn on each other because of... whatever this is."

"Same here," Zach chimes in, a hint of relief in his voice. "I'm glad we're talking about this, though. It means we can keep each other accountable."

"Exactly," I agree, struck by the gravity of the moment. "We need to be honest with each other, about everything."

"Agreed," Vaughn says, his green eyes filled with resolve. "We've come too far to let anything tear us apart now."

"Here's to the band," Zach adds, raising his glass in a toast.

"Cheers," we echo in unison, clinking our glasses together and sealing our pact in an echo of our earlier toast. As I drink, the warmth of the whiskey spreads through my chest, bolstering my confidence in our ability to navigate this new challenge.

As long as we stay honest and united, I know we can handle anything—even the irresistible allure of Dallas Graham.

Still, the weight of our conversation lingers heavily, swirling in the air like a ghostly presence. I stand up, needing space to breathe and process everything we've just laid bare. My guitar beckons to me from its stand like an old friend.

"Guys, I'm going to work on some new material," I announce as I grab my guitar.

"Sounds good," Vaughn nods, understanding the need for space. "We'll be here if you need anything."

"Thanks," I mumble before retreating to the back of the studio.

As soon as my fingers touch the cool strings of my guitar, a familiar warmth spreads through me, connecting me to the instrument that has always been a safe haven. I close my eyes, taking a deep breath, and let my fingers dance across the frets, weaving a melody that mirrors the turmoil churning within me.

"Damn these feelings, damn this desire," I whisper, briefly working on lyrics as I pour my conflicted emotions into every note, every strum. The chords resonate with the ache in my chest, giving voice to the fears and desires that threaten to consume me.

My fingers move faster, driven by the urgency of my thoughts, and the music intensifies, building to a crescendo that leaves me breathless. In that moment, clarity strikes like a bolt of lightning, illuminating the truth I've been searching for.

"Burn Notice is not just about the music... it's about us," I mutter, realization dawning on me. Our success relies not only on talent, but on our ability to navigate the complexities of our emotions, to find balance amidst the chaos.

I continue playing, the melody transforming into a hopeful anthem, reaching for that connection we all crave.

"United we stand," I murmur, the words weaving themselves into the fabric of my song. "Through highs and lows, we won't let go."

I play until my fingers ache, the music washing over me like a cleansing wave, carrying away the doubts and fears that have plagued me. It's not going to be easy—I know that. But as long as we stay honest and united, there's nothing we can't overcome.

"Here's to us," I whisper, striking one final chord before letting the music fade into silence.

With newfound resolve, I rejoin Vaughn and Zach.

"Guys," I begin, my voice steady and full of conviction. "I've been thinking—our success isn't just about our talent.

It's about our ability to stay connected through…well, through everything."

"Absolutely," Vaughn agrees.

"That's easy," Zach says. "No matter what happens, we put the band first."

"Deal," I say without hesitation, and I swear to myself that nothing will tear us apart.

Not even Dallas Graham.

6

ZACH

We're a solid week into rehearsals. The sun filters through the windows of our rehearsal space, casting rays on Dallas as she sits behind her drum kit. Her blonde hair cascades over her shoulders, creating a halo effect that makes it hard to look away. She grips the drumsticks with ease and begins to play, her eyes focused, yet glimmering with mischief. My fingers strum the chords on my guitar, but I can't help watching her.

"Let's take it from the top!" Fender calls out, breaking me from my reverie.

As we dive into the song, I notice how effortlessly Dallas syncs her rhythm with ours. The energy she brings to the band is undeniable—a burst of freshness, like opening a window in a stuffy room. And it's not just her skill; there's something about her presence that lights us up. I admire her talent, realizing that she could be the key to elevating our music to new heights.

"Nice work, everyone," she says, flashing a smile that

sends a flutter through my chest. The warmth of desire surges through me, and I'm surprised by its intensity.

"You're killing it on that solo, Zach," Dallas compliments me, further fueling my attraction to her.

"Thanks. You're really making those drums come alive," I say, trying to sound casual while my insides twist with conflict.

I know that pursuing a romantic relationship within the band could have serious consequences not only for our friendship, but also our musical chemistry.

But as I watch Dallas, her laughter filling the room like a melody, I can't deny my growing feelings for her.

"Hey Zach, you okay?" Vaughn asks, his voice pulling me back to reality. "You seem a bit distracted."

"Uh, yeah, I'm fine. Just lost in thought," I say, forcing a smile.

As the rehearsal goes on, I find myself torn between wanting to get closer to Dallas and fearing the disruption it could cause within the band—especially since we all pretty much promised not to pursue anything.

Besides, I've always been the mediator, striving for harmony, and the thought of jeopardizing that weighs heavily on me.

"Let's wrap it up for today," Fender finally suggests, wiping sweat from his brow.

As we pack up our gear, my mind races with questions. Would pursuing Dallas be worth the risk? If I give in to my desires, am I sacrificing the very thing that brought us together—our shared love for music?

"Great job today, guys," Dallas says cheerfully, slinging her bag over her shoulder. "I'll see you all tomorrow."

"See you," I say, watching her walk away, a mix of longing and fear swirling inside me.

The sun dips below the horizon as I lean against the brick

wall of our practice space, my heart heavy with the weight of my thoughts. The cool evening air brushes against my skin, doing little to quell the warmth that spreads through me when I think about Dallas.

"Hey man," Fender says, joining me outside, his guitar case slung over his shoulder.

"Hey," I say, offering a small smile, though it doesn't quite reach my eyes.

"Something's bothering you," he observes, leaning against the wall beside me.

I let out a deep sigh. "It's Dallas," I admit. "I like her. More than I should."

Fender's eyes search mine for a moment before he nods. "Yeah, I get it. She's talented, gorgeous, and she's got this energy—it's hard to resist. But we need to remember what's at stake here."

"I know," I say, running a hand through my hair. "Everything we've worked for could fall apart."

"Exactly," Fender agrees. "We can't afford to lose focus. Our friendship and this band mean everything to us. So, we prioritize those shared goals above everything else."

Despite the truth in his words, I find it difficult to ignore the way my heart aches at the thought of denying my feelings for Dallas. But I know Fender is right—we have to put the band first.

"IslandFest is our chance to save our career," I say, steeling my resolve—and I'm talking to myself even more than I'm talking to Fender. "We need Dallas to make it happen. I'll do whatever it takes to ensure we're successful, even if it means keeping my distance from her."

"Good," Fender says, clapping a hand on my shoulder. "We're in this together. Remember that."

As we head back inside, I push my personal desires aside and focus on the ultimate goal—our band's success.

THE NEXT MORNING, IN MY SMALL APARTMENT, I PACE BACK and forth.

Today, I've decided to take the initiative to get to know Dallas on a personal level, find a way to connect with her that goes beyond our mutual love for music.

Not because I'm interested in her—the opposite, in fact. I'm hoping I'll be able to push my attraction to her to the side if I get to know her better.

As friends.

Or so I tell myself.

"Hey," I say, approaching her hesitantly after rehearsal. "I was wondering if you'd like to grab some coffee with me? You know, just hang out and talk?"

Her blue eyes widen in surprise, but she quickly recovers and flashes a bright smile. "Sure. That sounds great."

We walk together toward a nearby café, and our conversation flows easily as we discuss our shared interests and dreams. I learn that she grew up here in Denver, just like I did, and that we both have a passion for exploring the outdoors. We share our favorite hiking spots and agree that there's nothing quite like the feeling of reaching the top of a mountain after a grueling climb.

Shit. The more I get to know her, the more I like her.

As we sit across from each other in the cozy café, sipping our hot drinks, I admire her fiery spirit and sense of adventure. It's easy to see why she has had such an impact on our band—she truly is a force of nature.

"Zach," she says suddenly, her gaze turning serious. "I wanted to ask you something. Are you…worried about what might happen between us? You know, romantically?"

I freeze, caught off guard by her blunt honesty. But I decide to confront my fears head-on.

"Truthfully, yes," I admit, my voice barely more than a whisper. "But it's not because I don't want it. It's because I'm afraid of what it could do to the band. To our friendship."

"Me too," she confesses, her eyes filled with the same mix of fear and longing I've been feeling.

I take a deep breath, bracing myself for what I'm about to say. "So, we need to talk about it. The potential consequences of pursuing a romantic relationship. It could impact our music, the band's dynamics. Maybe even our individual growth as artists."

Dallas nods in agreement, looking thoughtful. "You're right. As much as I don't want to admit it, we can't just pretend there won't be any repercussions."

We spend the next hour hashing out our concerns, dissecting every possible scenario and its potential impact on both our personal lives and the band. It's a difficult conversation, but one that feels necessary—a way for us to navigate these treacherous waters together.

Dallas reaches across the table to place a hand on mine. "No matter what happens between us, I want you to know that I care about you—and I care about the band, too. We'll figure this out, okay?"

I gaze into her eyes, feeling a sense of calm wash over me. "Yeah," I say, squeezing her hand. "We will."

As we leave the café and head our separate ways, I know that we've taken an important step toward understanding each other better.

As we wrap up another intense practice session. I watch Dallas as she tosses her blonde hair out of her eyes, sweat beading on her brow and a satisfied smile playing across her lips.

"We're really starting to gel," Fender says with genuine enthusiasm, clapping his hands together.

"Agreed," Vaughn chimes in, his green eyes shining with newfound confidence. "Dallas, you've got a killer rhythm going on. It's really pulling everything together."

"Thanks," she replies, flushing with pride. "And can I just say, Vaughn, your bass lines are blowing my mind. You've got some serious talent."

As I observe the exchange, it's clear that Dallas has had an effect on both Fender and Vaughn. They seem as drawn to her as I am, their attraction growing with each passing day. And it's more than just physical—her presence has reinvigorated our music and given us all a renewed sense of purpose. The energy she's brought to our group is like a spark, igniting a fire that had been smoldering for too long.

"Hey Zach," Vaughn murmurs, pulling me aside after practice. "Are you all right? You look like you've got something on your mind."

I hesitate for a moment, unsure whether to confide in him. But I know that I can trust him. "Well, it's just... I'm worried about what might happen if things get complicated between any of us and Dallas."

Vaughn studies me intently, searching my gaze for answers. "You mean, like what's happening between you and her?"

"Exactly," I admit. "But it's not just me—I can see the way you and Vaughn look at her too."

"True," Fender concedes with a sigh. "I guess we're all feeling that pull. But we can't let it mess with our focus."

"Right," I agree, taking a deep breath.

"We'll keep an eye on things," he says, "make sure everyone stays grounded. We've got a lot riding on this comeback."

As the days go by, I find myself stepping up as a source of

stability for the band. When emotions run high or tensions threaten to boil over, I offer a listening ear and a voice of reason, helping to defuse any potential conflicts.

And then, in a moment of clarity, it hits me: our success hinges on our ability to adapt and evolve.

It's not about avoiding complications or suppressing our emotions—it's about embracing the uncertainty and challenges that come with working with Dallas.

We need to trust in our shared passion for music to guide us toward our ultimate goals.

"Hey Zach," Dallas calls out one day after practice, her blue eyes dancing with mischief. "We ready to face whatever comes our way?"

A smile spreads across my face as I realize just how much she's come to mean to me—to all of us. "Yeah," I say. "We can handle anything."

And I truly believe it.

VAUGHN

The pulsing beat of my heart echoes in my ears as I watch Dallas from across the room, her laughter infecting everyone around her.

We're taking a break from rehearsing, and though I should be focusing on our upcoming gig in downtown Denver—a practice run for IslandFest—all I can think about is her. The way her eyes crinkle when she smiles, the glint that seems to always linger there, and the light brush of her hand against mine earlier today.

It all sends a shiver down my spine.

She stands up and heads toward the bathroom in the back of the rehearsal space.

"Hey," Fender drawls, snapping me out of my thoughts. "You look like you're deep in thought over there. Everything okay?"

"Uh, yeah," I mutter, rubbing the back of my neck.

My mind races with the internal conflict I've been grappling with for days now—my attraction for Dallas clashing with the raw fear of exposing my vulnerabilities and PTSD. How could I ever subject her to the emotional baggage I carry? Would pursuing a relationship even be worth the potential turmoil it could bring?

Zach chimes in, his dark brown eyes searching mine for any sign of discontent, "You've been kinda distracted lately, man. Something bothering you?"

"It's just... Dallas." I blurt out before I can stop myself. "I mean, I don't know if it's just me, but there's something about her that's hard to ignore."

Fender's eyes meet mine, understanding flashing through them. "We've noticed it too," he says, glancing at Zach who nods in agreement. "She's got this energy, this pull on all of us."

"Right," I say, feeling a strange relief knowing I'm not alone in my feelings. "But what do we do about it? I mean, we're all attracted to her, but..."

Fender leans back in his chair, crossing his arms. "It's a tricky situation, no doubt about it," he concedes, furrowing his brow. "But we can't ignore it either. We need to figure out how to navigate this without tearing each other—or the band —apart."

"We've been through so much together, guys," Zach interjects. "We can handle this too, as long as we include Dallas."

"Are you suggesting we talk to her about our feelings?" I ask.

"Maybe not all at once," Fender says with a snort. "But yeah, I think we should consider it."

I nod slowly, my mind racing. My heart pounds in my chest as I imagine what could happen if I opened up to Dallas, laid bare all the scars and darkness that haunt me.

"Whatever we decide," I say quietly, looking between my two closest friends.

The dimly lit practice room feels charged with energy, the

remnants of our conversation still buzzing through the air as Dallas makes her way back into the room.

I pick up my bass guitar and begin to play, seeking solace in the familiar weight of the instrument. My fingers glide across the strings, each note resonating within me, drawing out the tangled emotions swirling inside.

"Let's try that new track again," Dallas calls out from behind her drum kit, her blonde hair pulled back into a messy ponytail. The playful sparkle in her blue eyes belies the seriousness with which she approaches her craft.

As I play, I pour all of my conflicting feelings into the music—my fears, my desires, the ever-present specter of my PTSD. The low rumble of the bass seems to echo the turmoil in my chest, and for a moment, I feel better about it all.

My gaze flits to Dallas as she begins to drum, her movements precise and powerful. She's completely in her element, her raw talent commanding my attention. I find myself captivated, watching as she masterfully controls the rhythm, driving us forward with unyielding determination.

"Looking good!" Fender shouts over the music. "Keep it up!"

Dallas flashes us a grin, sweat beading on her forehead as she continues to play. Her energy is infectious, invigorating us all with renewed vigor. It's no wonder we've all been drawn to her—she's magnetic and exhilarating to be around.

But with that attraction comes uncertainty, as well as the potential for heartache. The tension among us all has only grown since she joined the band, and I worry that our shared desires for her will threaten the stability we've worked so hard to build.

"God, let's take a break," Zach says, bringing me out of my thoughts. He wipes his brow with the back of his hand, his eyes heavy with exhaustion. At this point, we've been practicing for hours, and it's starting to take its toll on all of us.

"Great job, everyone," Dallas adds, hopping off her stool and stretching her arms above her head. "That was our best run yet."

"Thanks to you," I say before I can stop myself. She looks over at me, surprise registering in her eyes before she smiles warmly.

"Hey, we're a team," she replies.

I smile back, even as my heart twists with apprehension. She's right—we're a team, bound together by our love for music and our shared dreams. And if we want to protect that bond, we'll have to keep our priorities and emotions in check.

"Let's call it a night," I suggest, setting down my bass guitar with a sigh. "We've made some great progress today."

"Agreed," Fender chimes in, already packing up his gear. "Rest up, everyone. Only a few more days before we hit the island."

As we leave the practice room, I steal one last glance at Dallas, still radiant even after hours of hard work. My attraction to her is undeniable, but so too are my fears. Only time will tell if we can find a balance between our desires and our responsibilities, continue chasing our dreams without losing ourselves in the process.

THE SUN SETS OVER THE DENVER SKYLINE, CASTING A WARM glow across the rooftop of my apartment building. I lean against the railing, taking in the view as I sip on my beer, feeling the slight chill of the evening air.

It's moments like these that allow me to quiet the storm within and find some semblance of peace. But tonight, my thoughts are still consumed by Dallas—her smile, her laughter, and the energy she brings to the band.

"Mind if we join you?" Fender asks, stepping onto the rooftop with Zach in tow—they each carry a bottle of beer, the three of us having ended up here after practice.

"Of course not," I say, making room for them at the railing. We stand in silence for a few moments, watching the city lights flicker to life as darkness settles in.

"You've been a bit off lately," Zach says to me. "Seems like it's more than just Dallas. Is everything okay?"

Inhaling deeply, I decide it's time to confide in my friends. "I've been struggling with my PTSD again," I admit, my voice cracking slightly. "And with Dallas around... I don't know—it just seems like I'm asking for trouble."

Fender places a reassuring hand on my shoulder. "Hey, we're here for you, man."

"You're stronger than you give yourself credit for," Zach adds. "We've all got our own demons to face."

He's right—and I know they'll be there for me if I need them.

We spend the evening reminiscing and laughing, but as I lay in bed later that night, my mind drifts back to Dallas.

The thought of pursuing a relationship with Dallas both excites and terrifies me. Would she be the catalyst for growth that I desperately need, or would she become another obstacle to overcome?

As sleep beckons me, I silently vow to approach this whole issue with a clear mind.

For now, that's all I can do. And maybe that will be enough.

THE SUN IS SETTING OVER THE DENVER SKYLINE AS I WALK into the studio the next day, the orange and pink hues painting a canvas across the sky. I take a deep breath to steady my nerves before stepping inside, knowing Dallas will almost certainly have already arrived.

"Hey," Dallas greets me with an easy smile when she sees me enter. She's adjusting her drum set, her blonde hair pulled back in a loose ponytail, strands framing her face.

"Hi," I say, trying to sound casual as I lean against the wall, watching her work. "How are you doing?"

"Pretty well, thanks," she says, pausing her adjustments to look at me. "I love playing with you guys... it's everything I've wanted." She pauses. "Sometimes I feel bad about ending up here because of the other drummer…"

I nod. "I get that.

Dallas's expression grows sympathetic, and I notice how her blue eyes seem to hold a world of understanding. "I can't imagine what you've been through, but I'm here if you ever want to talk about it."

"Thanks," I say, feeling warmth spread through my chest at her offer. "I appreciate that."

Our conversation shifts to more lighthearted topics, but I can't shake the protective instincts that have begun to bubble up inside me. The band's stability is fragile, and yet I keep weighing the risks of getting involved with her against our shared dreams.

The attraction between us is undeniable, but is it worth the potential fallout?

8

The pulsing rhythm of my drumsticks on the snare reverberates through the rehearsal space, sending exhilarating waves of energy as I lock eyes with each band member, making mental notes of their individual strengths and quirks as we allow the music to wash over us like a tidal wave of creative force.

I know I can add to Burn Notice, help make it a better band.

But only by connecting with each of the men.

And not just in the way I've started fantasizing about at night...

I shake off my lustful thoughts and focus back in on the music.

During a break, I approach Fender.

God, he's sexy, I think—but I remind myself to tread carefully. "You know, your voice has this amazing power to draw people in," I tell him sincerely, then add, "Just remember that you're not alone up there."

His gaze holds mine for a moment longer than necessary, then nods. I can feel the heat rise in my cheeks, but I push it aside, focusing instead on the task at hand.

Next, I find Vaughn nursing a bottle of water, lost in thought. I've come to learn that beneath his stoic exterior lies a whirlwind of emotions, fears, and insecurities. "Hey," I say softly, not wanting to startle him. "You absolutely killed it on the guitar today. Don't let anything hold you back, okay? We believe in you."

His eyes meet mine, and he gives a small smile. "I appreciate that."

Lastly, I approach Zach, who's busy fiddling with his bass. He's a natural-born jokester, always ready with a quick wit and a flirty remark. I've come to enjoy our playful banter, but today, I want to have a genuine conversation.

"Zach," I say, placing a hand on his shoulder. "You're an incredible musician, and we all know it. But if you ever feel like you're struggling or need someone to talk to, don't hesitate to reach out to me, okay?"

He looks up at me, startled. "Thanks."

As the days tick by and we count down to IslandFest, I continue to foster these connections, listening intently as each band member shares their concerns and fears.

And the more I get to know them, the more my bandmates tug my desires in different directions.

But for now, I choose to focus on the present—on the thrill of playing together, the promise of IslandFest, and the magic that happens when we get together.

―――――

THREE DAYS BEFORE WE LEAVE FOR THE FESTIVAL, I STEP INSIDE the rehearsal space, feeling a buzz of excitement. My eyes immediately fall on Vaughn, his strong hands plucking at the bass guitar strings with intense concentration. The way he loses himself in the music sends shivers down my spine.

"Hey there," I say softly. "You're sounding amazing today."

"Thanks," he murmurs, a slight blush coloring his cheeks. Our eyes meet for a moment, and electricity charges the air between us. As I reach out to adjust one of the dials on his amp, our fingers brush against each other, sending a jolt of heat through me.

Then I notice the tension in his shoulders. "Is everything okay?"

"Yeah," he replies, hesitating for a moment before adding, "just dealing with some stuff." I can sense the vulnerability lurking just beneath the surface, the weight of his PTSD from the bus crash threatening to pull him under.

"Remember, you don't have to go through this alone," I say gently, offering a comforting hand on his shoulder. He nods, gratitude shining in his dark green eyes, and a strange warmth spreads through my chest.

I return his smile and move across the room to where Zach is tuning his own guitar. His dark hair falls into his eyes as he strums, and I grin at the playful smirk that spreads across his face when he catches sight of me.

"Hey, stranger," he teases—it's been less than ten hours since we ended our rehearsal the night before—as he leans against the wall. "Come to check out my mad skills?"

"Of course," I laugh, playfully bumping his shoulder with mine. "I can't resist witnessing such amazing talent."

"Watch and learn then," he says with a wink, launching into an impressive riff that leaves me grinning in appreciation.

"Okay. You might be almost as good as you think you are," I say, eliciting a chuckle from him. Our gazes lock, and a thrill of excitement flutters up my spine as I recognize the growing desire between us—the way my heart races when he's near, the spark of chemistry that ignites whenever we touch.

"Careful now," he says, leaning closer. "Wouldn't want to inflate my ego too much."

"Oh, I think your ego can handle it," I shoot back, feeling the heat of his body next to mine.

We share a moment of charged silence, the air thick with the unspoken question of what might happen if we let ourselves explore this connection further.

But I know we both understand the risks involved.

"Maybe after IslandFest?" I suggest coyly, offering a solution that keeps the door open, but respects the boundaries we've set for ourselves.

"Maybe what after IslandFest?"

Like he doesn't know what I'm saying.

I roll my eyes. "Maybe you'll actually be as good as you think you are."

He snorts. "Yeah, right."

He's still grinning as I step away from him, the anticipation of what could be simmering beneath the surface.

As I steal glances at Vaughn and exchange playful banter with Zach, I wonder if one of these connections might evolve into something more—and whether the risks might just be worth taking.

But how could I ever choose just one of them?

They're all hot as hell—and I want them all.

THE NEXT DAY, FENDER GETS TO REHEARSAL BEFORE ANY OF us. I'm the next to arrive, and as I walk in, he strums his guitar. His fingers dance along the frets, effortlessly coaxing out a melody.

"Mind if I join you?" I ask, approaching him with a smile.

"Of course not," he replies. "Take a seat."

As I sit down beside him, the magnetism between us exerts its force—an energy that seems to crackle in the air, igniting our every interaction. I know it's dangerous territory, but I can't deny the intensity of our connection.

Of course, that's true with all three of them.

"Your guitar playing is incredible, you know," I tell him. "You have a real gift."

"Thanks," he says, a hint of vulnerability flickering across his face. "It's been my saving grace, in more ways than one. Especially since the bus crash."

I know Vaughn's PTSD is a result of the crash, but none of them have talked about it much.

I think they'd all feel better if they didn't keep it bottled up inside.

"Tell me about it?" I say softly as I place a comforting hand on his arm.

Fender takes a deep breath, then begins to open up about the loss of their drummer, the guilt he carries, his struggle to trust others.

"Look, we all have our demons," I tell him gently. "But what's important is that we don't let them hold us back. We need to live life to the fullest—even if it means taking risks sometimes."

Like I'm one to talk.

I shove my inner critic down.

I can deal with my hypocrisy later.

Fender gazes at me, his eyes filled with desire. "But sometimes it's hard to know if the risks are worth taking."

"Isn't that what life is all about?" I challenge him, leaning in closer. "Taking chances and seeing where they lead us?"

"Maybe," he admits, his voice barely above a whisper as our faces draw nearer.

For a heartbeat, I'm certain he's about to kiss me.

Before we can cross that line, however, the door to the studio bursts open, and the other band members walk in, laughing and joking. Fender and I quickly pull away from each other, trying to maintain a sense of professionalism despite the lingering tension between us.

"Hey, everyone," Fender announces, clearing his throat as he gets back into leader mode. "Let's get this rehearsal started. Two days to go."

As we dive into practice, I steal glances at Fender, wondering what might have happened if we'd had more time alone together.

But for now, I tell myself that my heart races not because I want all three of them…but with the thrill of being part of this talented group.

My thoughts are a jumbled mess, consumed by my undeniable attraction to each one of them: the unspoken connection with Vaughn, the flirtatious repartee with Zach, and the smoldering intensity of Fender.

"Hey Dallas," Vaughn calls out, snapping me back to reality. "Wanna run through that new beat again?"

"Sure thing," I say, settling into my drum throne and gripping my sticks with determination. As I watch him strum his guitar, tattoos peeking out from under his rolled-up sleeves, his quiet strength and vulnerability draw me to him.

I glance up to catch Zach watching me watch Vaugh, and for an instant, it feels like there's an underlying tension, a spark of chemistry waiting to ignite. I struggle to remind myself of the potential consequences for the band's dynamics if we were to explore our desires any further.

"Break time," Fender says, his voice commanding and authoritative. He takes a seat next to me, close enough that I can feel the heat radiating off his body. We exchange a knowing glance, and a shiver runs through me.

"Everything okay?" Fender asks.

"Just thinking about IslandFest."

"Same here," he says, his eyes searching mine for a moment before looking away. I can tell there's more on his mind, but now isn't the time to delve deeper into our personal feelings.

As we continue with rehearsal, I try to focus solely on the music and the camaraderie we share.

But as we break for the day, I wonder what the future holds for me and my relationships with these three amazing men. The risks are undeniably high, and the consequences could be devastating, both personally and professionally.

But fuck, it would be an amazing ride—while it lasted.

9

FENDER

The heat hits me as soon as I step off the van, a warm embrace from the tropical sun.

Burn Strategy has arrived at IslandFest.

I squint against the brightness and catch sight of Vaughn and Zach to my right, their eyes wide with excitement. The air buzzes with anticipation, carrying the distant thump of drums and the hum of thousands of voices.

"We made it," I say, grinning widely.

"Damn right we did." Zach claps me on the shoulder. "Let's make this fucking rock, huh?"

"Absolutely," Vaughn agrees.

I take a deep breath, inhaling the salty tang of the ocean mixed with the aroma of sizzling food from nearby stands.

The atmosphere is intoxicating, a blend of vibrant energy and raw musical passion that makes my heart race. My fingers twitch with the urge to play, adrenaline coursing through my veins like an electric current.

"Let's get our gear set up," I say to the guys, trying to

maintain some semblance of control over my enthusiasm. "We've got a show to put on."

We've got a major performance the last night of the festival, but Ezra's booked us in at a couple of local bars—starting tonight. He's determined for us to make the best of this chance.

As we navigate the throngs of musicians and fans, I can't shake the mix of excitement and nervousness bubbling in my chest. This place is a playground of temptation—the talented musicians, the stunning scenery...and the beautiful women.

We're here to rebuild our reputation, I remind myself—not to indulge in distractions. Yet despite my resolve, there's one distraction I'm worried I won't be able to resist.

Dallas.

"Hey, Fender?" Zach nudges me as we're checking into our hotel. "You okay, man?"

"Uh, yeah," I mutter, forcing a smile. "Just...thinking about the show. You know how it is."

"Sure," Vaughn chimes in, a knowing look in his eyes that suggests he's not entirely buying my excuse. But he doesn't press, and for that, I'm grateful.

As we head up to our rooms, Dallas passes by me in the hall, her fingers trailing across my upper arm, and I shiver.

———

THAT NIGHT, AS WE MAKE OUR WAY TO OUR GIG, I LET MY GAZE wander over the sea of fans hanging out all over the island.

And when we walk into the bar, I realize a surprising number of those fans have come out to this otherwise nondescript bar on the island specifically to see Burn Notice.

It's not the kind of crowd we're hoping to draw to our main-stage show, but it's a crowd, nonetheless. The bar is bursting at the seams.

Their adoration hums in the air, and a surge of confidence washes over me. This is what I live for.

I've missed this.

We were so close to hitting it big right before the bus crash.

But then David's death derailed everything.

This is for you, man, I think.

Time to put all our rehearsals into action.

But as much as I try to focus on setting up, thoughts of Dallas keep creeping back into my mind. The memory of her touch lingers on my skin like a brand, searing and addictive.

Fuck, what am I doing?

I need to pull myself together, for the sake of the band, for our dreams...for my own sanity.

"Okay, Burn Strategy," I say, clapping my hands together. "Let's give these people a show they'll never forget."

"Damn straight!" Zach exclaims, pumping his fist in the air.

"Let's do this," Vaughn agrees, his voice steady and determined.

As the crowd roars and the first chords ring out, I close my eyes and lose myself in the music. For now, at least, I can push aside my desires and focus on what truly matters.

Our music.

THE NEXT DAY, THE SUN BLAZES DOWN ON THE SANDY SHORES of IslandFest as I make my way through the throngs of people, a guitar slung over my shoulder.

The scent of saltwater and sunscreen hangs heavy in the air, mixing with the unmistakable aroma of grilled food and spilled beer. I can feel the bass from a nearby stage vibrating through my chest, the energy it creates coursing through me like an electric current.

"Hey, Fender!" calls out a fellow musician, his dreadlocks bouncing as he waves me over. "Saw you last night. Man, you guys killed it up there!" I recognize him as Billy, the bassist from KillSwitch.

"Thanks, dude," I say, clapping him on the back. "Can't wait to see your set tonight."

"Appreciate it, man" he says, grinning. "We should jam sometime."

"Definitely," I agree, already envisioning the magic that could be created by combining our unique sounds.

Especially now that Dallas has given us a harder beat.

As we part ways, I continue to weave through the crowd, taking in the sights and sounds of IslandFest.

It's a melting pot of talent and passion, a place where music reigns supreme and its disciples gather to worship at its altar. And in this moment, I am both priest and parishioner, offering up my devotion in every chord and lyric.

"Excuse me," comes a soft, feminine voice from behind me. "Are you Fender from Burn Strategy?"

I turn to see a beautiful woman with sun-kissed skin and eyes the color of the sea. A faint blush colors her cheeks as she holds out a pen and a crumpled flyer. "Could I get your autograph?"

"Of course," I say, signing my name with a flourish. She beams at me, clearly thrilled by our brief interaction, and I smile back.

The attention is intoxicating, a heady reminder of the power I wield when I step on stage, guitar in hand.

"Thank you so much," she gushes before disappearing back into the crowd.

As I continue to move through the sea of admirers, my confidence swells with each autograph and selfie. But beneath it all, there's a nagging sense of longing—a yearning for something, or someone, that can't be satisfied by the adulation of strangers. My thoughts drift to Dallas, her laughter echoing in my ears like a siren's call.

I shake my head, trying to banish the image of her from my mind.

But as another fan approaches, her eyes filled with heat, I wonder if there's more to life than just the pursuit of fame. And if maybe I'm ready to find out.

———

THE SUN SINKS BELOW THE HORIZON, PAINTING THE SKY IN hues of pink and orange as I wander away from the festival and along the shoreline, kicking off my shoes and allowing my feet to sink into the cool sand.

The day's events, a whirlwind of music and adoration, linger like a dream at the edge of my consciousness. I find myself drawn to the hypnotic rhythm of the waves, their soothing murmur offering a momentary reprieve from the chaos of IslandFest.

"Beautiful, isn't it?" a familiar voice says from behind me.

I turn to find Dallas standing there, the fading sunlight casting a golden halo around her blonde hair. The sight steals my breath away, rendering me momentarily speechless. She looks ethereal, like a nymph born from the sea itself.

"Dallas," I manage to choke out, taking a step toward her. "Yeah, it is."

She smiles, a hint of mischief dancing in her eyes. "Enjoying the festival so far?"

"Definitely," I say, my gaze flickering over her face, searching for any indication of the emotions churning within me. "How about you?"

"Absolutely loving it," she says, her smile widening as she

tucks a stray lock of hair behind her ear. "But I needed a break from all the excitement, and the beach seemed like the perfect place to escape."

"Same here," I admit, my heart racing as I close the distance between us. The heat of her body radiates against my skin, intoxicating me with its warmth.

"Good thing we found each other then," Dallas teases, her lips curving into a sultry grin.

Unable to resist the magnetic pull between us any longer, I lean in and capture her lips with mine.

The kiss is electric, igniting a fire that sweeps through my veins and consumes every ounce of self-control I possess. Dallas responds with equal fervor, her hands tangling in my hair as she deepens the embrace.

But just as I'm about to lose myself completely in the passion of our connection, Dallas pulls away, her eyes wide and filled with a mix of desire and uncertainty. "Fender...I—I can't," she stammers, stumbling back a step.

"Wait," I call out, reaching for her. But she's already turned and fled, leaving me standing alone on the beach, the taste of her lips lingering like a bittersweet memory.

Fuck, fuck, fuck.

What have I done?

I SPEND THE NEXT DAY WATCHING OTHER BANDS PERFORM— and although I know I should be drinking and partying, soaking up the music surrounding me, I find myself grappling with conflicting emotions.

The sun dips low in the sky, casting an ethereal glow over IslandFest, and I make my way over to the main stage, where KillSwitch is performing.

They're every bit as good as I remember. With every

strum of the guitars and beat of the drums, the energy pulsates through the air, a tangible connection between the band and the audience. The adrenaline rush of remembered performances fuels me, but underneath it all, I can't ignore the lingering memory of Dallas' lips pressed against mine.

"Great set, man!" Vaughn exclaims as KillSwitch steps off stage, sweat dripping from their brows.

"Thanks," Billy says, and I try to shake off my conflicting emotions.

"Hey," Dallas approaches, her eyes shining with admiration. "You guys were amazing."

"Thanks," Billy says, the high of the performance—and who knows what else—shining in his eyes.

I manage to smile even as my heart pounds at the sight of Dallas—I didn't know she was in the audience.

"Wanna party with us?" Billy asks.

I glance around at my own band members, and everyone nods.

We all end up back at the bar where we performed the night before, where KillSwitch and other fellow musicians have gathered to celebrate another night of successful performances.

I join the party, but my gaze never strays far from Dallas. And despite the lively atmosphere, I find myself lost in thought, contemplating the risks of pursuing a romantic relationship within the band.

"Are you okay?" Dallas's voice surprises me from behind.

"Of course," I lie, attempting to mask my internal turmoil. "Just thinking about our other gigs. And the main stage show. That's all."

"Understandable," she replies with a gentle smile. "You put your soul into the band. It's what makes you so captivating."

Her words send a shiver down my spine, a dangerous spark igniting in my soul. I wonder if our passionate exchange on the beach was merely a momentary temptation… or something deeper.

"Look," I begin, my voice low and hesitant. "About last night..."

"Maybe we should talk about it later," she interrupts, her cheeks flushed with color. "When we're both clear-headed."

"Right," I nod, taking a deep breath. As much as I crave her touch, her warmth, I know it's a bad idea.

"Enjoy the rest of the night," she says before slipping away, leaving me to grapple with my desires alone.

I am so fucking screwed.

But as I watch Dallas disappear into the crowd, one question remains: can I truly let her go?

10

ZACH

The next morning, Ezra calls to tell Fender we've been invited to fill in on a side stage for one of the bands that's a no-show. It's a short set, in the middle of the afternoon, but good exposure, anyway.

So now I stand watching the band playing before our set, amid the sea of eager fans and pulsating music. The scent of coconut sunscreen and sweat fills the air, intermingling with the intoxicating aroma of various food stalls.

Glancing around at all the people, I shiver with anticipation, my guitar strap resting heavy against my shoulder.

"Hey, Zach!" a voice calls out, snapping me back to reality. Turning, I spot a familiar face from The Grindstone Oracle, a tall, blond-haired guy named Ryan. He approaches me with a grin. "Dude! I didn't know you were going to be here! Burn Notice playing—or are you looking for a new band?"

"Ha! In your dreams, man," I say, clapping him on the shoulder. Our exchange is lighthearted. I'd almost forgotten how good it is to be in crowds like this, full of other musicians and music-lovers.

"Welcome back, then," he says, raising a beer in a toast before taking a swig. "You're looking good."

As we chat idly about our experiences at IslandFest so far, a couple of girls in bikinis walk by, glancing back over their shoulders at us.

I can't help but notice the way boundaries seem to blur in this atmosphere. There's an undeniable undercurrent of sensuality that sweeps through the festival, carried on the ripples of laughter and the heat of bodies pressed close together in the crowd.

It makes me think of her—of Dallas.

Shit. She's been occupying my thoughts more and more lately.

Her magnetic stage presence makes it impossible not to be drawn to her. I've seen the way she looks at me, her hazel eyes locking onto mine with a hunger that both excites and terrifies me.

But there's something deeper between us, something I can't quite put my finger on—a connection that goes beyond lust.

"Hey, Earth to Zach," Ryan teases, waving a hand in front of my face. "You still with me, man?"

"Sorry," I mutter, shaking off the distracting thoughts of Dallas. "Just got lost in thought for a second."

"Thinking about your chances of scoring tonight?" he asks, glancing after the girls and wiggling his eyebrows suggestively.

"Something like that," I say, my mind still reeling from the unbidden fantasies of what might happen between Dallas and me if we were to let our desires run wild.

Would it be worth risking everything for a taste of the forbidden?

Jeez, I'm being over-dramatic, I think, pulling my mind back to the present.

"Good luck out there," Ryan says with a knowing grin as he claps me on the back and heads off to join his own band-mates. As I watch him go, I wonder if he senses my internal struggle—if he knows that beneath my calm exterior lies a storm of conflicting emotions, threatening to consume me whole.

But whatever happens between Dallas and me will have to wait; after all, we're here to rock, and that's exactly what we intend to do.

The other band up on the stage ends their set, and the rest of my band shows up.

A cacophony of excited chatter, laughter, and the distant sound of guitars tuning fills the air as we prepare to take the stage. The sun is hot over the festival grounds, but a chill creeps up my spine, born of anticipation and unspoken desires.

"Okay, Burn Strategy!" Fender shouts, pumping us up before our performance. "Let's give them a show they'll never forget!"

I grip my guitar tightly in an attempt to steady my nerves. A sea of faces stares back at me from beyond the stage.

"Hey, you got this," Dallas says softly. She reaches out to squeeze my arm, and I struggle to swallow the lump that's formed in my throat.

"Thanks," I manage, praying that my voice doesn't betray the tempest of emotions swirling inside me.

As the first chords of our opening song ring out across the crowd, I focus all my energy on showcasing our talent and raw power. Each note is like a lifeline, grounding me in the moment and drowning out the siren call of desire that threatens to consume me.

"Feeling it, Zach?" Fender shouts into his microphone,

and I nod, doing my best to embrace the intensity of the music while keeping my darker fantasies at bay.

"Damn right, I am!" I yell back, strumming harder and watching as the audience jumps and dances along with us. It's exhilarating, this connection we share with our fans—but I wonder what it would be like to forge a similar bond with Dallas, to let the fire between us burn bright and untamed.

"Zach, solo!" Fender calls, snapping me back to reality. I launch into the intricate guitar work, letting my fingers dance across the fretboard as I strive to prove our band's worth—and perhaps garner some validation for myself in the process.

But even as I pour my heart and soul into the music, I steal glances at my bandmates, observing the shifting dynamics between us. The air seems charged with electricity, sparking with the tension of unspoken desires and hidden fears. It's clear that we're all grappling with our own demons, seeking solace in the music that binds us together.

As our set draws to a close, I allow myself a brief moment of introspection, pondering the impact of this festival on our relationships.

Can I continue to resist temptation, or is it only a matter of time before I give in to my overwhelming desire?

"Great job, guys!" Dallas exclaims as we step off the stage, her eyes shining with pride and something more. "We really brought it up there!"

I try to ignore the way my heart races in response to her proximity. As we make our way through the throngs of festival-goers, I can't shake the feeling that we're hurtling toward a precipice, teetering on the edge between friendship and something far more dangerous.

And as I watch Dallas disappear into the crowd, her laughter echoing in my ears like a promise of something yet to come, I wonder: when the time comes, will I have the strength to resist, or will I let myself be consumed by the fire?

———

A FEW HOURS LATER, THE SUN DIPS BELOW THE HORIZON AS I stand amidst the pulsating energy of the festival, the vibrant colors and infectious rhythms of the band on stage commanding everyone's attention. My gaze drifts to Dallas, who is lost in the music, her eyes closed and her body swaying in time with the beat. The sight of her like that stirs something deep within me, the hunger I've been trying to keep at bay.

"Damn, they're good," Fender shouts over the music, his admiration clear.

"Yeah," I agree, my mind still preoccupied with thoughts of Dallas and the boundaries we've set for ourselves.

"Hey, I'm gonna grab a drink! Want anything?" Fender asks, pulling me from my thoughts.

"Uh, no thanks, man. I'm good," I say, forcing a smile. In truth, my thirst lies elsewhere.

"All right, catch you later!" he yells before disappearing into the crowd.

The band reaches an emotional crescendo, and I watch Dallas, her expression mirroring the intensity of the music. It's like she's calling to me, beckoning me closer. I take a deep breath, steeling myself.

"Hey," I say as I approach her, my voice barely audible above the guitar riffs. "I need to talk to you about tomorrow's practice session."

"Sure, let's head somewhere quieter," she suggests, her blue eyes locking onto mine with a knowing look. We weave through the sea of dancing bodies, making our way to her hotel room where we can speak privately.

Once inside, I relay the information about the practice session, but my mind is elsewhere. I can't ignore the charged atmosphere between us any longer.

"Zach..." Dallas whispers, her voice soft and tentative. "Is there something else on your mind?"

I gaze into her eyes, searching for a sign that she feels the same electric pull that I do. The air between us crackles with intensity, and I know in that moment that I need to know her in every way possible.

"It's just... this festival, the music, everything," I begin, my heart pounding in my chest. "It's made me question our boundaries..."

"Maybe we should ignore those boundaries," she breathes, her gaze never leaving mine.

I can't resist any longer; I close the distance between us, pressing my lips against hers in a fiery, passionate kiss. Her body melts into mine, and for an intoxicating moment, nothing else matters but the taste of her and the heat of our desire.

"Zach," she murmurs against my lips, her hands tangling in my hair, pulling me closer. "I've been waiting for this."

"Me too," I confess, my voice barely a whisper. Our passion continues to build, fueled by the undeniable connection between us. And as we lose ourselves in each other's embrace, I wonder if breaking our boundaries was the right decision, or if it will ultimately lead to our downfall.

Moments later, my phone buzzes in my pocket—it's Fender's ringtone. I draw away from Dallas and pull the phone out.

"Fender," I say.

Dallas's eyes widen. "I need to go," she mumbles, then flees from her own hotel room.

Fuck. Did we make a mistake?

"Zach, where are you, man?" Fender's voice pulls me from my thoughts. "We're going to go see Frank Fen perform."

"Be right there," I say, taking one last look at the empty space where Dallas once stood. The taste of her lips still lingers on mine, a sweet reminder of our passionate kiss. My heart races, and the thought of losing the harmony within Burn Notice weighs heavily on my mind.

But there's no denying the fire that sparked between us— a fire that refuses to be tamed.

11

VAUGHN

I slandFest is alive with the rhythmic thumping of bass, electric guitars wailing, and impassioned vocals that weave a spell over the crowd. Frank Fen's a hell of a performer, and his new backup band rocks.

I can feel the vibration in my chest, as if the music is trying to tear me apart from the inside out as Frank finishes his set.

"Man, this is insane!" Zach exclaims, his dark eyes wide with excitement.

As we weave our way through the throngs of people, I notice the groupies closing in. They wear clothes that cling to their bodies like second skin, predatory gazes locked onto us. Their sweet perfume mixes with the sea air, creating an intoxicating blend that threatens to cloud my mind.

"Hey, boys," one of them purrs, sidling up to Zach and running her fingers along his muscular arm. "Wanna party?"

"Thanks, but not tonight," he says, flashing her his signature laid-back smile.

"Come on, don't be shy," another coos, attempting to wrap herself around Fender like a vine. He gently pushes her away, his gaze never leaving hers.

"Sorry, love. We got other things on our minds."

The groupies' attention turns to me, their advances more aggressive than before. But something inside me resists their call, and I manage to extricate myself from their grasps.

"Maybe some other time," I mutter, my thoughts elsewhere.

As we make our escape, I glance back at the women we left behind. They're beautiful, no doubt about that, but they're not Dallas.

And in that moment, I realize that we all turned down the groupies because we all want her—our tiny, strong, and mischievous drummer who has completely bewitched us.

"Fuck, guys," I say aloud, "this Dallas thing might be a problem."

"Tell me about it," Fender replies, his expression grim. "But what are we supposed to do?"

Zach gives a helpless shrug, his usual calm demeanor faltering under the weight of this revelation. "I don't know, man. But we can't let it affect the band."

"Yeah," I say, my hands shaking with the intensity of my desire for Dallas. "We have to figure this out."

As I walk away from Zach and Fender, the IslandFest crowd seems to close in around me. The press of bodies and the cacophony of voices threaten to trigger my PTSD, but I push the anxiety aside, focusing on finding Dallas.

When I finally spot her, she's standing behind one of the stages. She's flirting with the lead singer from another band, her blue eyes sparkling with mischief as they share a laugh. A fierce pang of jealousy surges through me, and I'm stunned by its intensity.

"Hey," I call out, my voice low and rough as I approach

them. They both turn to look at me, their laughter fading. "Dallas, can I talk to you for a minute?"

"Sure thing," she says, gently disengaging herself from the other man's grip on her waist. As we step away from him, I notice the lingering scent of his cologne still clinging to her skin.

"What's up?" she asks, her eyes searching mine for answers.

"Look, I just... I need you to know something," I stammer, struggling to find the right words. I reach out and brush a strand of hair from her face. "I saw you with that guy, and it made me realize how much I want you. How much we all want you."

Her eyes widen at my admission, and for a moment, I worry that I may have gone too far. But then, her lips curl into a slow, seductive smile.

"Is that so?" she purrs, stepping closer to me until our bodies are mere inches apart. "And what do you plan on doing about it?"

"Right now?" I say, the heat between us building to a fever pitch. "This."

Leaning down, I capture her lips in a fiery, passionate kiss. The world around us fades away as the force of our desire consumes us both, and I lose myself in the taste of her —sweet like tropical fruit and salty like the ocean breeze. Her hands tangle in my hair, pulling me even closer, while my own grip on her waist tightens, unwilling to let her go.

As we finally break apart for air, I realize that no matter how complicated our situation may become, I am certain of one thing: Dallas is worth fighting for.

"Vaughn," she breathes, her eyes locked onto mine, "I don't know what's going to happen with all of us, but right now, I want this. I want you."

"Then let's not worry about the future for now," I whisper, pressing another searing kiss to her lips.

THE DOOR TO MY HOTEL ROOM CLICKS SHUT BEHIND ME, THE cool air inside a stark contrast to the heat outside. As I lean against the door, my mind races. The taste of Dallas lingers on my lips like tropical fruit and an ocean breeze, making it impossible to forget.

"Shit," I mutter under my breath, running a hand through my hair.

What did I get myself into?

My thoughts drift to Zach and Fender, knowing they both want her too.

I drop my gaze to the floor, staring at the patterned carpet as I consider the potential consequences. It's not hard to imagine jealousy and resentment tearing us apart, but I'm drawn to her like a moth to a flame.

"Maybe it won't be that bad," I whisper, attempting to convince myself. "We're all adults, right? We can handle this."

Despite my words, the knot in my stomach remains.

The nagging feeling refuses to leave me, and I realize it's not just about the band. My own fears and insecurities are gnawing at me. How can I fully embrace love and trust when I'm still haunted by the past?

How can I move forward?

"Vaughn?" A voice calls from the hallway, snapping me out of my thoughts—Zach, worry coloring his tone. "You okay in there, man?"

"Fine," I call back, forcing a smile into my voice. "Just needed a minute to think."

"All right, well, we're meeting up with Fender at the pool

if you want to join," he offers, giving me an out. But I know what I need to do.

"Thanks, but I'll pass," I say, my voice steady. "I've got some things to sort out in my head first."

"Okay," Zach hesitates before adding, "but we'll be there for a while."

"Sure, dude. Thanks."

As soon as I hear his footsteps recede down the hallway, I walk over to the window, looking out at the vibrant island landscape. The sun casts a warm glow over the palm trees and sandy beaches, offering a sense of tranquility that feels distant from the turmoil inside me.

"Maybe it's time to face my demons," I murmur to myself, taking a deep breath. If I want a chance with Dallas, and if I want the band to survive, I need to confront my own fears.

"All right," I say, clenching my fists. "You can do this." And as I stand there, surrounded by the beauty of the island and the promise of a new beginning, the first stirrings of hope take root within me.

THE SUN IS SETTING OUTSIDE OUR TEMPORARY REHEARSAL space as I pick up my bass guitar. The weight of it in my hands feels familiar and comforting, a tether anchoring me to something bigger than myself. I take a deep breath, centering myself before we begin our final practice before the main show.

Zach and Fender arrive, and we exchange nods.

When Dallas walks in a moment later, the tension level in the room ratchets up several notches.

As we start playing, I lose myself in the rhythm, my fingers finding their way across the strings as if guided by some unseen force. I pour every ounce of my heartache, frustration, and longing into each note, embracing the catharsis that comes with playing.

"Man, you're on fire tonight," Fender remarks.

"Thanks," I say. This is what it's all about—the music, the connection, the raw energy that binds us together.

By the time we're done, the sun has set. The sound of waves crashing against the shore provides a soothing backdrop as we pack up our instruments after practice.

"Great job, everyone," I say, wiping the sweat from my brow. "I think we're ready for this show."

"Definitely," Zach agrees, grinning. "We're going to blow them away."

As I glance around, though, I notice one person is missing. "Where'd Dallas go?"

"She went to grab some drinks," Fender replies, his voice casual but his eyes betraying a flicker of something deeper— longing, perhaps. Jealousy at the thought of her with someone else, even if it's just getting drinks, shoots through me.

"Hey, you guys good?" Dallas calls out, appearing in the doorway, carrying a tray filled with colorful cocktails.

Both Zach and Fender perk up at her arrival, and I realize that they feel the same way about her as I do.

But instead of feeling threatened or jealous, I find myself thinking...*why not? Why can't we all have her?*

An image of her naked, writhing under all our hands flashes through my mind.

Fuck, dude, I tell myself. *That's depraved.*

"Perfect timing," I say, flashing her a smile as she hands me a drink. "Just what we needed."

But I can't get the depraved idea out of my mind, and my cock twitches in response.

"Cheers to a great practice," Dallas says, raising her glass.

We clink our glasses together and take a sip, the sweet, tangy liquid doing wonders for our parched throats.

"So, what are your plans for tonight?" she asks us all. "You guys up for wild adventures, or are you going to be responsible adults and get some sleep before the big show?"

"Wild adventures, of course," Zach says with a playful grin. "What would IslandFest be without a little fun?"

"Count me in," Fender adds, his enthusiasm evident.

"Sounds like a plan," I say, feeling a thrill at the thought of spending more time with Dallas. "Let's make tonight one to remember."

In the end, though, we watch a couple of bands and then walk along the beach, laughing and stumbling after a few too many drinks.

I steal glances at Dallas. The curve of her smile when she laughs, the way her body sways as she walks—it's intoxicating, and I find myself wanting her more and more.

As I watch Zach and Fender, both vying for her attention in their own ways, I marvel at the fact that I don't care if they want her too.

All that matters is that I get to be a part of her world, share in the laughter and passion that she brings to our lives.

And if that means sharing her with my bandmates...so be it.

12

The hot sun beats down on the IslandFest crowd, their excitement as redolent as the coconut scent of sunscreen and the underlying smell of sweat and alcohol as they swarm around me.

I grin and sign autographs, pose for photos, and soak in the love Burn Strategy fans shower us with. The gig at the bar and the show on the side-stage made a splash, and it's intoxicating, this energy that courses through the air, electrifying the atmosphere.

I think of channeling it into my performance, the drumsticks flying over the skins like extensions of my own body.

"Thanks for coming out!" I call to a group of girls who squeal and snap more pictures. Adrenaline pumps through my veins like liquid fire, stoking the embers of desire within me.

After a while, though, it's exhausting, so I grab a rum punch and find a quiet spot under a palm tree to drink it.

As the festival buzz inside my head dies down, I reflect on

the passionate kisses I've shared with each of my bandmates. The memories come crashing over me, a tidal wave of raw emotion that threatens to consume me whole.

I close my eyes, remembering the taste of Vaughn's lips, the way his warm green eyes seemed to pierce my soul as he pulled me closer. His strong arms wrapped around me, shielding me from the world outside our embrace, and I felt an overwhelming sense of safety. The emotional anchor of our band, he held me steady when I thought I might lose myself to the chaos of desire.

But God—Zach. His laid-back demeanor and calming presence. The moment our mouths met, I knew we were kindred souls, drawn to one another by an unspoken understanding. His dark brown eyes, always filled with genuine warmth, made me feel seen and cherished. And yet, there was that flicker of doubt, that fear of rejection lurking just beneath the surface, mirrored in my own hesitation.

And the wild abandon of my kiss with Fender, the intensity of our connection like a thunderstorm rolling across the sky. He always seemed to see right through me, understanding both my deepest desires and most hidden fears.

My heart thunders as I consider the problems I've set myself up for. Can I continue to walk this delicate tightrope, craving passion and intimacy while trying to maintain the balance we so desperately need?

The distant crash of waves and laughter of festival-goers fill the air, and I close my eyes, allowing the sounds to wash over me.

I ponder my own desires. Each connection felt unique, yet equally intense. Can I truly choose just one of them without tearing the band apart?

"Hey Dallas, mind if I join you?" Vaughn's voice breaks through my thoughts. He sits down beside me on the sand.

Zach approaches next, flopping down on the other side of

me with his usual exuberance. He grins widely, his emerald-green eyes sparkling with mischief. "What are you guys talking about?"

"Life outside the band," I say, welcoming him into the conversation.

"Shit. Does that even exist?" Vaughn asks with a laugh.

I guess it shouldn't surprise me that Fender finds us too. He hesitates for a moment before sitting down, and I can see the vulnerability in his posture.

And though I still don't have all the answers, one thing is clear: I can't bring myself to give any of them up.

I want them all.

So, for now, I embrace the uncertainty.

As the conversation flows, the atmosphere becomes lighter, and the pressures of IslandFest seem to melt away.

———

LATER THAT NIGHT, ALONE IN MY HOTEL ROOM, THE MEMORIES of the passionate kisses with my bandmates swirl in my mind.

The heat of desire rises within me, and I can no longer resist the urge to touch myself.

I slide my hand beneath the waistband of my panties, imagining each of their hands on my body, their lips trailing fiery kisses across my skin.

God. All three of them.

At once.

The fantasy is delicious.

Forbidden.

Taboo.

Depraved.

And I want it more than I've ever wanted anything before in my life.

I want them to play my body like they play their instruments.

As I delve into the fantasy, I picture Vaughn's strong arms holding me tight, Zach's gentle caresses sending shivers down my spine, and Fender's intense gaze as he watches us all with a hunger that mirrors my own.

Slowly, deliberately, I bring myself closer and closer to the edge, the sensations building within me like a crescendo of longing and desire.

As I slide my finger across my clit, I imagine it's Fender's tongue—then Vaughn's, then Zach's.

Heat pools in my core, and I slip a finger inside myself, wishing it were one of my bandmates.

And as I finally reach my climax, I cry out, overwhelmed by the intensity of my feelings for these three incredible men who have come to mean so much more than just bandmates.

Then, the image of all of them finding a place in my body flashes through my mind and my orgasm crashes over me. I barely manage to bite back a scream.

In the afterglow, I lay there, catching my breath.

Afterward, though, I can't lie still.

I might have orgasmed, but my body knows that my own touch isn't what I've been craving.

I want them to touch me.

All of them.

13

R ays of light reflect off mics and amplifiers and sweat drips down my forehead as I watch another band perform.

David would have loved this—the balmy ocean breeze, the taste of salt in the air, and the way music pulses through every inch of the island. His laughter echoes in my mind, a haunting reminder of his absence.

I push through the crowd, working my way to the edges, then bending over with my hands on my knees, gasping for breath.

"Hey, are you all right?" A gentle voice interrupts my thoughts, and I look up to find Dallas standing before me. Her concern shines in her eyes, as if she can see right through my carefully constructed façade.

"Y-yeah," I stammer out, trying to regain control of my emotions. "Just needed a moment to catch my breath."

"Mind if I join you?" she asks softly. And though every

instinct screams at me to push her away, to keep her from seeing the raw vulnerability simmering beneath the surface, something about her presence feels like an anchor—grounding me amid the chaos of my own mind.

"Sure," I whisper, unable to meet her gaze. Her warmth radiates through the small space between us, and for the first time in what feels like forever, I allow myself to exhale.

The oppressive heat of the crowded festival begins to suffocate me, and I find myself longing for some quiet respite.

"But let's get out of here," I say.

She nods, and slipping away from the throngs of people, I lead her to the practice space Ezra rented for Burn Notice. The moment I step inside, the deafening noise of the outside world fades into a distant hum.

"Is there anything you want to talk about?" Dallas asks gently, and despite the walls I've built around my heart, I consider the offer. Dallas has a way of making me feel safe, as if I could reveal my deepest secrets without fear of judgment.

"Maybe," I admit, hesitating just a moment before continuing. "But not right now."

I drop down to a stool and study Dallas's face, her expressive blue eyes filled with concern and curiosity. A bead of sweat trickles down my temple, a testament to the oppressive island heat—and Dallas's presence. I exhale slowly, weighing the risks of opening up to her about something so raw and painful.

"Okay," I reluctantly agree, my voice barely above a whisper. "It's just... it's about our former drummer."

Dallas nods, her gaze never leaving mine as she takes a seat on an amplifier across from me. Her lithe legs crossed at the ankles, her shoulders bare beneath thin straps of her sundress. I swallow hard, trying to focus on the words I need to say rather than the way she stirs something primal within me.

"His name was David," I begin, my voice cracking slightly as I force myself to continue. "He was like a brother to me and losing him... it broke something inside of me. I feel responsible for his death."

Dallas's eyes soften, a wave of empathy washing over her features. She reaches out, placing a comforting hand on my knee. The warmth of her touch sends a shiver down my spine, but there is also solace in the contact.

"I'm so sorry," she murmurs, giving my leg a gentle squeeze. "But you can't blame yourself for something that was beyond your control."

I take a deep breath, feeling the weight of the secret I've been carrying finally starting to lift. "I know that logically, but it doesn't change the guilt. It's like I owe it to him to make this band everything he believed it could be."

"David would be proud of you and how far Burn Notice has come," Dallas offers, her voice steady and reassuring. "He wouldn't want you to torture yourself like this."

My chest tightens at her words. "Maybe you're right," I concede, finally allowing myself a glimpse of hope. "But it's just so damn hard sometimes."

"Let me be there for you," Dallas says, her eyes meeting mine with a determination that is both fierce and tender. "You don't have to carry this weight alone."

In this moment, surrounded by the humid island air and the remnants of my shattered heart, I find myself willing to take a chance on Dallas, on the possibility of healing.

And as we sit there, tangled in the aftermath of my confession, I can feel the faintest flicker of hope beginning to burn within me.

The weight of my confession seems to hang in the air

between us, but as the seconds tick by, I find myself feeling lighter than I have in months. Dallas' understanding gaze lingers on me, and the compassion in her eyes makes it clear that she doesn't judge me for my guilt or my grief.

"Thank you," I murmur, my voice hoarse with emotion. "I didn't realize how much I needed to let that out."

Dallas reaches out to squeeze my hand.

The warmth of her touch sends a shiver down my spine, igniting a storm of desire that I've been trying to suppress since the moment I first laid eyes on her. My pulse quickens as I take in the sight of her flushed cheeks, the swell of her chest as she breathes deeply, and the way her lips seem to beckon me closer.

"Kiss me," I hear myself say before I can stop the words from escaping. It's a plea, a demand, and a surrender all rolled into one, and when Dallas gazes back at me, I see the same hunger reflected in her eyes.

"Are you sure?" she asks, her voice barely more than a whisper, giving me one last chance to retreat from this precipice we're standing on.

"More than anything," I say, my heart pounding so hard it feels like it might burst through my chest.

I don't know what's changed since she ran from me on the beach, but as if pulled by some magnetic force, our mouths collide, and I lose myself in the intensity of the kiss. Our tongues dance together, exploring each other's depths, as I run my fingers through her soft blonde hair, desperately trying to memorize every curve and contour of her body.

With each passing second, the fire within me burns brighter, fueled by the taste of her lips and the feel of her body pressed against mine. The world outside our secluded sanctuary fades away, leaving only the heat between us and the unspoken promise of what's to come.

"God, you're amazing," I murmur against her lips as our

passionate embrace deepens. Every nerve in my body screams for more of her touch, as if she holds the key to a part of my soul that's been locked away for far too long.

"Let's get these off," Dallas whispers breathlessly, her fingers expertly working to unbutton my jeans. I follow suit, assisting in the removal of her own clothing. My hands tremble with anticipation as we finally stand naked before one another.

"Damn," she says, her eyes drinking me in, "you're absolutely gorgeous."

I smile at her words. "You're not so bad yourself," I tease, gently pulling her down to the floor next to me.

A sultry laugh escapes her lips as she wraps her legs around my waist, inviting me closer. Our bodies press together hungrily, seeking solace in each other's warmth and desire. I explore her form with my hands, my fingers tracing the curves and dips of her body like the strings on my guitar. It's as if playing her body is another form of music—one that sends shivers down my spine and sets my heart ablaze.

"Please," she gasps, her voice laced with need.

"Fuck, yes," I say, kissing her passionately before moving lower, trailing wet kisses along her collarbone, between her breasts, and down her stomach. Her breath catches when I reach her center, pausing briefly to look into her eyes— seeking permission to move forward.

"Go ahead," she whispers, a mixture of excitement and trust shining in her gaze.

I take a deep breath and allow my tongue to taste her. The electrifying sensations that pulse through me as I focus on her pleasure are unlike anything I've ever experienced.

Slicking my tongue around her clit, I savor her flavor— hot and musky and undeniably Dallas. Her soft moans and gasps punctuate the air, driving me to bring her closer and closer to the edge.

"God… you're incredible," she murmurs, her fingers gripping my hair as her hips rise to meet my eager mouth. The whole room feels charged with an electric intensity.

"Come for me," I urge, my voice a low growl as I increase the pressure and speed of my movements. "I want to hear you scream my name."

"Fuck, Fender!" she cries out, her body tensing as a powerful orgasm crashes over her like a tidal wave, leaving her breathless and trembling in its wake.

"Wow," she whispers, her eyes shining with emotion as she reaches down to pull me up to her level.

Dallas's heated gaze draws my attention, and our eyes lock. There's an unspoken understanding that passes between us—we've crossed a line we can't take back, and neither of us wants to.

"Let me return the favor," Dallas murmurs, her voice full of promise. She slides down my body, leaving a trail of fiery kisses in her wake. I suppress a shiver as she reaches my throbbing erection, her lips hovering just above it, teasing me with her proximity.

"Please," I beg, my voice barely a whisper.

And then her soft lips envelop my cock, sending shockwaves of pleasure through every fiber of my being.

"God," I groan, my hands instinctively finding their way to her head, guiding her movements. Her tongue dances around the head, flickering its way up and down my cock, driving me wild with need.

I don't know how much longer I can hold off.

"Damn, Dallas… you're so good at this," I pant, feeling my climax building like a storm on the horizon. I try to focus on anything but the sensations coursing through me—the steady rhythm of Dallas' mouth, the taste of Dallas on my lips mixing with a hint of salt from the island air—but it's impossible. I'm entirely consumed by her.

Dallas pulls away for a moment and I groan at the loss of her touch. "Come for me," she urges before bending back to her task. Her touch and her words combine to bring me to the edge of ecstasy. I can't hold back any longer.

I cry out, surrendering to the onslaught of pleasure as I reach my peak, my entire world narrowing to the connection between us. My cock jerks and throbs as I explode in her mouth, and she continues sucking me, taking the sensation even higher.

As the waves of my orgasm subside, I'm left gasping for breath, clinging to her as if she's my lifeline. Her mouth gentles and slows as she softly licks me, and I shudder.

Dallas smiles and pulls away, her blue eyes sparkling with satisfaction. "That was… intense."

"Intense is an understatement," I say, still struggling to catch my breath. We exchange a look that speaks volumes—acknowledging the depth of our connection and the new territory we've entered.

A voice sounds outside, and Dallas and I glance at each other, startled.

As we scramble to put our clothes back on, the door swings open, revealing another band entering the practice space.

"Hey, guys," the lead singer says with a knowing smirk. "Enjoying the practice room?"

"Um, yeah," I stammer, trying to sound nonchalant. "Just needed some time to… uh… work on a few things."

"Sure thing," he chuckles, clearly not buying our charade.

Dallas avoids eye contact with him as we hastily gather our belongings and make our exit. As we slip out of the practice space, a strange mix of embarrassment and satisfaction suffuses me.

"Guess we should be more careful next time, huh?" Dallas suggests, her eyes flashing with mischief.

"Next time?" I repeat, raising an eyebrow at her boldness.

She grins and links her arm through mine as we walk away. A slow smile spreads across my face as I realize that whatever comes next, one thing is certain—life with Dallas Graham will never be dull.

14

ZACH

A glow seems to emanate from Dallas as she emerges from the practice space, her arm linked with Fender—who's looking awfully pleased with herself.

They pause to talk with a group of festival-goers at IslandFest, and I admire her charisma. She has always had this magnetic pull that draws people in, and it seems to be working its magic now.

"Thanks so much for coming!" Dallas says brightly. "We hope you enjoy the show!"

Fender murmurs something to her. She nods and he takes off. I notice her cheeks are flushed, and she seems a bit hurried in her actions—like she's trying to put some distance between herself and the practice room. It only makes her more desirable in my eyes, and an unexpected surge of inspiration courses through me. This is the moment I've been waiting for—the moment when I need to take a chance and pursue my feelings for her.

As Dallas finishes up with the group, I take a deep breath and walk toward her, my heart pounding in my chest. My usual laid-back demeanor momentarily falters under the weight of the words I'm about to say.

"Hey," I call out, trying to sound casual. She turns around, her blue eyes locking onto mine with a mixture of surprise and curiosity.

"Zach! What's up?" She grins.

"Can we talk for a minute? Somewhere quieter?" I ask, glancing around at the crowd that's slowly forming near our practice space.

"Sure," she agrees, looking a little confused but still smiling. "Let me grab a drink first?"

We stop at a stand for drinks—she grabs one of her usual island-style rum punches, and I take a beer.

We walk toward the beach, where the sound of waves crashing against the shore drowns out the noise from the festival. I can feel my palms growing clammy as we reach a secluded spot, framed by swaying palm trees.

"Is everything okay?" Dallas asks with a frown.

"Yeah, it's just... I've been wanting to tell you something for a while now," I begin. The sound of my own heartbeat fills my ears, drowning out everything else.

It's now or never.

"Go on," she prompts, her eyes searching mine for answers.

Taking a deep breath, I muster up all the courage I have and say the words that have been on the tip of my tongue for far too long. "Dallas, I'm really attracted to you. More than that, actually. I've been trying to ignore these feelings for the sake of the band and our friendship, but I can't do it anymore."

A wave of vulnerability washes over me. My stomach churns with anxiety, and I brace myself for her response. But instead of laughter or rejection, I see a flicker of something else in her eyes—something that looks like desire.

But before she can answer, a young woman approaches me, her eyes wide with excitement.

"Zach Hayashi? Can I get your autograph?" she asks, thrusting a pen and a tattered festival flyer in my direction. A group of women hang back behind her, watching the interaction.

"Sure," I say, forcing a smile. With that, the other women swarm toward me, too.

Dallas leans in. "I'll be in my hotel room. Talk there?"

I blink as she walks away, and I quickly jot down my signature. Then I do it over and over again. The fans thank me profusely, but I barely hear their words—my thoughts are consumed by the image of Dallas' flushed face and the way her eyes seemed to hold a flicker of desire.

Letting out a frustrated sigh, I make my way toward the hotel. I need to know if what I saw in her eyes was real or just wishful thinking on my part. As I reach her door, my heart hammers against my chest, threatening to burst free. Drawing in a deep breath to steady myself, I knock.

The door swings open, revealing Dallas wrapped in a towel, her blonde hair damp and clinging to her neck. A cloud of steam billows around her, carrying the scent of her shower gel and making my head swim.

"I..." My voice catches in my throat as I struggle to form words. All I can think about is how close I am to her, how the heat from her body mingles with the warm island air, sending shivers down my spine.

"Come in," she says, stepping aside to let me pass. As I cross the threshold, she closes the door behind us, sealing us away from the world.

I reach out to brush a damp strand of hair from her cheek, marveling at the softness of her skin.

"I just couldn't wait any longer."

"Wait for what?" she whispers, her breath warm against my hand.

Taking a leap of faith, I lean in and press my lips to hers. The moment our mouths meet, it's as if a dam has burst within me, releasing all the pent-up emotions I'd been holding back for so long. I wrap my arms around her, pulling her closer, and feel her respond with equal fervor.

As we kiss, I let go of my reservations and embrace the passion burning between us. The taste of her lips, the warmth of her body pressed against mine—it's all-consuming, driving away any lingering doubts or insecurities. In this moment, there's only Dallas.

"Zach," she gasps when we finally break apart, her eyes wide and filled with wonder.

"Tell me you feel it too," I plead, my voice barely more than a whisper.

"I do," she admits, her cheeks flushed, and her gaze locked onto mine. "I've felt it since the moment I met you."

With Dallas's admission, something within me ignites, and I pull her to me again, our mouths crashing together with a hungry intensity. Our hands roam each other's bodies, exploring, teasing, stoking the fire that threatens to consume us both.

"Zach," she moans into my mouth, her fingers digging into my shoulders as her towel slips away, revealing her naked form. "Please... I need you."

"God," I groan, unable to tear my gaze from her, her blonde hair wild and damp, her blue eyes filled with desire. "You have no idea how long I've wanted this."

I lift her effortlessly, carrying her over to the bed and laying her down gently. The contrast of her soft skin against the crisp white sheets is intoxicating, and I can't resist running my fingertips along the curve of her hip, up her side, and finally cupping one of her breasts. She arches into my touch, a wanton sigh escaping her lips.

"Touch me," she begs, reaching for my shirt, tugging at the hem, urging me to remove it. I comply, discarding all my clothes and joining her on the bed, my body pressed against hers, our heat mingling in the sultry island air.

I slide my hand down to her pussy, finding her already hot and wet, ready for me.

I'm throbbing, aching with need for her.

"Now," she says. "Please."

I roll her under me, hovering above her for a moment before carefully, slowly, sliding my cock into her. She clenches around me, and my cock jumps in response.

Then I begin moving, pushing myself as deep into her as I can go before drawing out again.

Our lovemaking is slow and deliberate at first, our bodies moving together in a sensual dance that leaves us both breathless. But as our passion grows, so too does the urgency of our movements.

"Harder," she pants, her nails raking down my back, leaving trails of fire in their wake. "I need more."

I give her what she craves, my hips snapping against hers with a fierce intensity that has her crying out my name. We are lost in the tempest of our desires, consumed by an all-consuming lust that threatens to leave us shattered in its wake.

"Zach, I'm so close," she gasps, her body trembling beneath me.

"Let go," I urge her. "I've got you."

My words are enough to send her crashing over the edge, her hips jerking wildly beneath me, her voice crying out my name.

I feel the inner walls of her pussy flutter around my cock, squeezing me, and almost without warning, I come, erupting inside her, holding her tight against me as waves of pleasure roll through me.

Afterward, our bodies slick with sweat and our hearts pounding in tandem, I think that this is what I've been searching for my entire life: this wild, untamed connection that transcends everything else.

But even as the afterglow of our passion begins to fade, my thoughts drift to my bandmates. My loyalty to them is unwavering, but I know that this could be a problem.

Right now, though, I don't care.

HOURS LATER, MOONLIGHT BATHES THE ROOM IN A SOFT GLOW as I pull on my jeans, stealing glances at Dallas, who lies sprawled across the bed. Her golden hair fans out over the pillow, framing her face like a halo. My fingertips graze the smooth skin of her arm, and I marvel at the passion that has unfolded between us.

"Hey," she murmurs, her blue eyes blinking sleepily. "You're leaving?"

I nod, swallowing the lump in my throat. "I should go before anyone notices I'm gone."

"Right," she whispers, disappointment flickering in her gaze. "The band."

"Promise me," I say, pausing at the door, "that we'll figure this out, together."

"Promise," she replies, her voice barely audible.

As I step into the dimly lit hallway, the door clicks softly behind me. The silence envelops me like a shroud, and I exhale, my breath shaky. My heart races as the significance of our encounter dawns on me—there's no going back to the way things were.

My mind buzzes with thoughts of the band as I wander

through the hotel, the sound of waves crashing against the shore echoing in my ears. Could our passion bring the music we've created together crumbling down?

"Zach?" a voice calls out, pulling me from my thoughts. I turn to see one of our crew members approaching, concern etched on his face. "You okay, man?"

"Fine," I force a smile. "Just needed some air."

"All right," he says, eyeing me warily before heading back in the direction of the festival grounds.

As I continue walking, the tropical breeze dances around me, teasing the palm trees and rustling their leaves. It's then that I realize my determination to keep Dallas in my life. In her embrace, I found something I'm unwilling to let slip through my fingers.

"Zach!" a group of fans shout, waving excitedly as they spot me from a distance. Forcing a grin, I head their way, prepared to sign autographs and take photos. But as I engage with them, my thoughts remain rooted in that hotel room, in the warmth of Dallas' touch.

15

The sun rises over the island, casting a warm golden glow through the curtains as I slowly wake up. The band's pivotal performance is the day after tomorrow. The pressure weighs heavily on me, and my muscles tense with anxiety.

But I get up and pull on clothes, planning to go out to take a walk on the beach.

Maybe I should start doing yoga every day, like Zach does.

Hell of a thing for a rock star to do.

But then—Sting's been doing tantric yoga for ages.

I laugh at the thought and head outside.

"Hey!" Dallas's voice calls me, and I glance over to find her heading toward the beach, too. "Mind if I join you?"

"No problem."

I realize I would never deny her anything.

The sound of crashing waves creates a soothing rhythm as we walk along the shoreline.

Dallas walks beside me, her blonde hair dancing in the breeze, her blue eyes reflecting the vibrant colors of the morning sunlight.

"Vaughn," she says gently, breaking the silence that had settled between us. "You've been really quiet. What's going on?"

A deep breath fills my lungs with salty air, steadying my nerves as I prepare to share my deepest fears with her. In this moment, surrounded by the beauty of nature, I find the courage to open up about the darkness that haunts me.

"Ever since the bus crash, I've been struggling," I confess, my voice barely audible over the roar of the ocean. "I can't shake the memories, the nightmares...it's like I'm still trapped in that twisted metal, screaming for help."

Dallas stops walking and turns to face me, her eyes brimming with concern. "I didn't realize it was that bad," she admits, reaching out to place a hand on my arm. "Why didn't you say something sooner?"

"Because I didn't want to burden anyone else with my problems," I say, avoiding her gaze. "Especially not you."

"Vaughn, you're not a burden," she insists, catching my chin and forcing me to look at her. "We all care about you, and we want to help you through this."

Her touch sends a shiver down my spine, and I fight the urge to pull her closer.

"Sometimes, I feel like I'm trapped in a dark room, unable to escape," I say, my voice trembling. "The walls close in, and I can't breathe. The panic is suffocating."

She pulls me into a tight embrace. "You're not alone in this. Okay?"

"Okay," I agree, allowing her warmth to seep into my soul, providing a small measure of comfort.

As we stand there, wrapped in each other's arms, for the first time in what feels like forever, I feel complete.

The ocean's rhythmic lapping against the shore echoes in my ears as Dallas and I continue to stand there, her arms wrapped around me protectively. I lean into her touch, closing my eyes and breathing in her scent.

"Vaughn?" Dallas whispers softly, her breath tickling my ear.

"Y-yeah?" I stammer, my heart pounding in my chest.

"Can I... kiss you?" she asks hesitantly, as if unsure how I'll react.

"Please," I breathe, giving her permission to bridge the gap between us.

Her lips meet mine gently at first, as if testing the waters. But when I don't pull away, she deepens the kiss, her tongue exploring the contours of my mouth with a passion that ignites my own desire. My hands find their way to her waist, pulling her closer as our bodies meld together.

We break apart for a moment, gasping for air as we take in each other's flushed faces. And then, without a word, Dallas leads me by the hand back toward the hotel, where we go to my room.

Once inside, the world beyond the four walls ceases to exist. We lose ourselves in a whirlwind of passion and longing, desperate to claim one another completely.

The air in the hotel room is thick with anticipation, the scent of our mingled desires forming an almost palpable cloud around us. I can't take my eyes off Dallas as she stands before me, her sundress hugging her body like a second skin. With every beat of my heart, my need for her intensifies, and I know there's no turning back now.

"Are you sure about this?" I ask her, needing to hear her confirmation one more time. Her piercing blue eyes lock onto mine, filled with a raw hunger that matches my own.

"Absolutely," she breathes, her voice sultry and low. "I want this, Vaughn. I want you."

That's all I need to hear. My hands reach for the thin straps of her sundress, fingers trembling slightly as I slide them down her delicate shoulders. The dress falls away from her body, pooling at her feet like a discarded dream. She stands there, exposed and beautiful, the soft glow of the bedside lamp casting a warm light across her curves.

My mouth waters as I take in the sight of her nipples, hard and inviting. I lean down, capturing one between my lips, sucking gently, savoring the taste of her. A moan escapes her, and it sends a shiver down my spine, igniting a fire deep within me. I switch to the other nipple, lavishing it with equal attention, losing myself in the pleasure of giving her pleasure.

"Vaughn..." she whispers, her fingers tangling in my hair, urging me closer. I can feel the heat radiating from her body, her desire for me mirroring my own. It's overwhelming, and I can't get enough.

"Touch me," I urge, my voice husky with need. She hesitates for only a moment before placing her small hand on my chest, her fingers tracing the ridges of my muscles. The sensation is electric, sending jolts of pleasure coursing through me. Her touch is tentative at first, as if she's afraid to break me, but I crave more, need her to feel the strength of my desire for her.

"Go on," I encourage her. A wicked grin tugs at the corners of her lips, and it's as if a switch has been flipped. She presses her hand harder against my chest, slowly trailing it down my body, exploring every inch of me with tantalizing precision.

As her fingers trace lower, I can feel my resolve crumbling, my self-control slipping through my grasp like sand through a sieve. My breath hitches in my throat, and I know it's only a matter of time before I'm completely lost to the passion we're igniting together. And God help me, I want nothing more than to drown in it.

My mind races with the intensity of our connection, my fingers tracing patterns on her thighs as she continues to explore my body. Her breathing grows heavier, her blue eyes clouding with desire.

"Vaughn, please," she whispers, the desperation in her voice sending a shiver down my spine. That's all the encouragement I need.

I glide my hand up her inner thigh, feeling the heat radiating from her core. She gasps in anticipation, and I can't help but smirk at her reaction. "You want this, don't you?"

"Yes," she breathes, her fingers digging into my shoulders.

"Tell me what you need," I demand, my voice low and commanding.

"Touch me," she pleads. I won't make her wait any longer.

My hand finally reaches its destination, and I'm rewarded with a moan that sends a jolt of pleasure straight to my groin. My fingers dance across her sensitive flesh, teasing her mercilessly, building her desire until she's trembling beneath my touch.

"Vaughn, I'm so close," she whimpers, her hips moving instinctively against my hand. I can feel the tension coiling within her, ready to snap.

"Let go, Dallas," I urge her, my touch relentless. "Show me how much you want this."

With a cry, she surrenders to the onslaught of sensation, her body shaking with the force of her release. The sight of her, so lost in pleasure, is enough to bring me to the brink myself. But it's not over yet—not by a long shot.

"Your turn," she pants, her eyes alight with mischief. With surprising strength, she pushes me back onto the bed, straddling me as she positions herself above me.

"Ready?" She grins wickedly, and despite the lingering tremors of her climax, she's clearly not finished with me yet.

"Always," I reply, my voice heavy with desire. As Dallas takes control, I can't help but marvel at the woman above me —strong, fierce, and unapologetically passionate.

All that matters is the woman on top of me and the fire we're stoking together. And as I give myself over to the heat of our connection, I know that there's nowhere else I'd rather be.

The way Dallas looks down at me, her blonde hair cascading around her flushed face, is hot as hell. She leans in and captures my lips with her own, the taste of pure desire on her tongue. I can't help but be swept up in the moment, the electricity that pulses between us igniting a fire inside of me.

"Vaughn," she breathes against my ear as she grinds herself against me, teasing me with tantalizing friction. "I need you."

"God, Dallas," my voice comes out husky and raw, "I need you too."

As I reach down to position myself at her entrance, I'm struck by how perfectly we fit together. The connection we share goes beyond just the physical; it's an emotional bond that has developed between us like the harmony of our instruments on stage. With each thrust, I feel the barriers around my heart crumbling, revealing a vulnerability I've buried deep within for so long.

"Vaughn, don't hold back," she whispers, her nails digging into my shoulders. "I want all of you."

Her words are the catalyst that sets me free. I let go of my fears, my insecurities, and surrender to the passion that engulfs us. Our bodies move in perfect sync, a rhythm as natural and powerful as the beat of her drums.

"Vaughn, I... I'm close," she gasps, her body trembling beneath mine.

"I'm ready," I assure her, my own pleasure building to a crescendo.

As if on cue, her body tightens around me, her eyes locked onto mine as she spirals into another earth-shattering orgasm.

As I feel Dallas's body quiver with the aftershocks of her release, my self-control begins to unravel. I grit my teeth, fighting back the urge to surrender to the pleasure threatening to consume me whole.

"God, Vaughn," she breathes against my ear, her voice a sultry whisper that sends shivers down my spine. "You're so... incredible."

"Fuck, Dallas," I manage to gasp out, my hips still grinding against hers as I chase the edge of oblivion. Her hands glide over my sweat-slicked skin, tracing patterns of desire that only fuel the fire raging within me.

My heart races, pounding in my chest like the drums we both know so well, the rhythm a testament to our connection—both on stage and off. I can't help but get lost in her eyes, those deep pools that seem to see straight through me, into the very depths of my soul.

"Vaughn, baby, let go," she murmurs, her hands pulling me closer. "I want to feel you come."

And with a final thrust, I finally allow myself to succumb to the pleasure coursing through me, my release washing over me like a tidal wave, drowning out the world around us.

"Ah, fuck!" I cry out, my entire being focused on the ecstasy consuming me, as I empty myself into her, our bodies connected in the most primal and intimate way possible.

As we lay entwined in the aftermath of our lovemaking, a mixture of emotions washes over me. Relief at having finally given in to my desires for Dallas mingles with fear and vulnerability at the thought of what this intimate encounter might mean for our future.

"Vaughn?" Dallas murmurs, tracing patterns on my chest as she rests her head against my shoulder.

"Yeah?" I manage to say, my voice hoarse from our earlier passion.

"Was this... okay? I don't want you to regret anything," she says, genuine concern lacing her words.

"It was more than okay," I whisper, pressing a tender kiss to her forehead. "It was everything."

"Vaughn," she says, her eyes searching mine for answers, "I know things have been complicated lately, with your PTSD and the pressure we're all under. But I want you to know that I'm here for you, no matter what."

Her words wrap around me like a warm embrace, offering a sense of safety that I've been craving for so long.

"Thank you," I murmur, my hand instinctively reaching for hers.

"Promise me something," Dallas says, rolling over to face me more directly. "Promise me you won't try to face your demons alone. Let us help you."

My instincts have always been to protect, not burden those I care about with my struggles. But in her eyes, I see that my well-being is just as important to her as it is to me.

"I promise," I say, squeezing her hand.

"Good," she says, her lips curving into a smile that ignites a familiar warmth in my chest.

THE SALTY OCEAN BREEZE RUFFLES MY HAIR AS I STAND ON THE balcony of Zach's room. The waves crash against the shore, their rhythmic pattern matching the pounding of my heart.

My thoughts are consumed with Dallas, the way her laughter dances in the air.

"Hey," Zach calls from behind me, pulling me from my reverie. "Fender and I are heading to lunch. Ready to go?"

"Sure," I agree, following him inside where Fender waits by the door, his blue eyes bright with anticipation. As we walk along a sandy path toward a small café, I wonder if it's time to open up to them about what happened between Dallas and me.

I can't control how they react, but I can take control of my own emotions and desires.

And right now, all I want is to explore the fiery passion that burns between Dallas and me.

16

T he sun beats down on my skin as I make my way across the white sand, a mixture of excitement and apprehension churning in my stomach. Today's lunch with the band has been planned for days now, but recent events have left me feeling uncertain about how it will go.

"Hey, Dallas!" Fender calls out, waving me over to their table at the beachside café. The salty breeze ruffles his dark hair as he grins, and my heart skips a beat.

"Hi guys," I say, sliding into the empty seat next to Vaughn. His muscular arm brushes against mine, sending a shiver up my spine. The tension in the air is almost tangible, thick enough to cut through with a knife. I know that the recent events have stirred up emotions among the band members, and I worry about what might happen today.

"Can I get you a drink?" Zach asks, his green eyes fixed on me with desire. I bite my lip, trying to shake off the butter-flies in my stomach.

"Uh, sure, just a water for now, thanks," I say, forcing a smile. Thoughts of our tangled relationships race through my mind, and I know I'm responsible for the mounting tension among us all.

As Zach heads to the bar to grab my drink, Vaughn leans in closer to me, his warm breath tickling my ear. "You okay?" he murmurs, genuine concern lacing his deep voice. I nod, swallowing hard.

"I'm fine," I say, taking a deep breath and attempting to steady my racing heart. "Just a bit nervous about everything, I guess."

Vaughn squeezes my hand reassuringly, his calloused fingers rough yet comforting. "We'll figure things out. We always do."

I glance around the table, my eyes meeting those of each band member in turn. I love them all—it's undeniable, and I can't bear the thought of losing any one of them.

But how do we navigate these uncharted waters without tearing ourselves apart?

The tension in the room is like a thick fog that clings to my skin and weighs on my conscience. I can't escape the feeling that something significant is about to transpire, and as I watch the band members exchange uneasy glances, I know it's only a matter of time before the dam bursts.

"Look," Fender begins, his brown eyes clouded with worry, "we need to talk about... well, everything."

I can feel the blood draining from my face, leaving me cold and vulnerable. This is the moment I've been dreading.

"We all care about you," Vaughn continues, his voice tense, "but we're not blind. We know what's been going on between you and each of us, and it's causing problems."

As I look into the eyes of these men whom I've grown to love, I see their fear, their jealousy, and their desire. My heart aches at the thought of causing them pain, but I can't deny my own feelings for them either.

"Guys..." I begin, my voice barely audible above the hum of conversation around us. I take a deep breath, summoning every ounce of courage I possess. "I know this is hard, and I understand why you might be feeling threatened by the situation. But I can't choose between you. I just can't."

Their expressions shift from concern to shock, as if my words have struck them like a physical blow. Fender looks down at his hands, rubbing them together nervously, while Zach's mouth hangs open in disbelief. Even Vaughn, who has always seemed so strong and unshakable, appears lost for words.

"Here's the thing," I continue, steeling myself against the wave of emotions threatening to overwhelm me. "I believe that our connections—our love for one another—can actually make us stronger. But we have to be willing to confront our own insecurities and trust each other completely."

The words pour out of me, raw and unfiltered, as I lay my heart bare in front of them. My chest tightens with anxiety, but I know that this is a conversation we can no longer avoid.

"Each of you brings something unique and special to my life, and I don't want to lose any of you," I confess, my voice trembling. "But we need to find a way to make this work, without tearing the band—or ourselves—apart."

Vaughn's eyes widen, his fingers gripping the edge of the table, and Fender runs a hand through his dark hair, visibly struggling to process my words. Zach leans back in his chair, arms crossed defensively over his chest.

"None of this... none of this makes any sense," Vaughn stammers, his voice barely more than a whisper. "How can you expect things to stay the same between us?"

I press on, determined not to let fear dictate the outcome of this conversation. "I'm not saying it will be easy," I admit, twirling a strand of my hair around my finger. "But I think part of the reason you're all struggling with jealousy is that you haven't faced our own fears and insecurities."

"Look," I say, meeting each of their gazes in turn, "you each have your own demons. Fender, you're afraid of letting people close because you've lost someone important before. Zach, you're worried about rejection and losing the bond you share with the band. And Vaughn, you're battling PTSD and feel like a relationship would burden others with your struggles."

Silence hangs heavy in the room as they absorb my words, the weight of their vulnerabilities laid bare. The waves crashing against the shore outside serve as a stark reminder of the island paradise surrounding us, a place where emotions run high, and secrets are impossible to keep.

"Guys, we've been given an incredible opportunity here," I continue, gesturing at the sunlit beach visible through the window. "We're living our dream, playing music together and enjoying the beauty of this place. But if we want to protect what we've built, we all need to confront our fears and work through them—together."

Fender's eyes fixate on mine, the intensity of his gaze almost overwhelming. "And how do you propose we do that?" he asks, his voice husky with emotion.

"By trusting one another," I say firmly, my voice growing stronger with conviction. "By accepting each other—flaws and all."

"Can we really make this work?" Zach asks hesitantly, his dark brown eyes searching mine for reassurance. "Can we really have it all?"

"Only if we're willing to fight for it," I answer, the fire in my soul burning brighter than ever before. "But I know we can do it, because our bond is stronger than any jealousy or conflict."

As the truth of my words sinks in, I see a glimmer of hope igniting in their eyes, like the first rays of sunshine breaking through storm clouds. It's a fragile, delicate thing, but it's there—a tentative first step toward a future none of us had ever dared to imagine.

My heart pounds with a mixture of determination and vulnerability as I lean against the rustic wooden table, its surface worn smooth by countless meals shared. The scent of saltwater and coconut oil hung heavy in the humid air, a constant reminder of the paradise we find ourselves in. "We have something special here," I say, my voice soft but unwavering. "But if we let jealousy and conflict take hold, it'll only lead to our downfall."

"Is it even possible?" Vaughn asks, his green eyes clouded with doubt as he runs a hand through his tousled hair.

"I believe it is," I answer, feeling the weight of my words settle on my shoulders. "But we've got to talk about it. If you're jealous, ask yourself why. What are you afraid of losing? What's driving your possessiveness? Work through those feelings instead of letting them fester and poison what we have."

Their expressions shift as they absorb my challenge, uncertainty giving way to contemplation. The sound of waves crashing against the shore drifts through the open windows, punctuating the silence that hangs between us.

"All right," Zach finally says, his dark brown eyes meeting mine. "Let's give it a shot. We owe it to ourselves, and to each other, to at least try."

"Agreed," Vaughn adds, his gaze steady as he offers a tentative smile.

"Fine," Fender concedes, crossing his arms over his chest but nodding in agreement.

A surge of relief washes over me. It won't be easy, but I believe in us.

"Guys," I say, my voice quivering slightly. "I want you to know that I have my own fears and uncertainties about being with all of you. But... it's also my dream."

They exchange glances, then turn to me, curiosity and surprise etched on their faces.

"Your dream?" Fender asks skeptically, his brow furrowed.

"Yeah." My eyes flicker between them, seeking under-standing. "I've never been one for convention, and I've always followed my heart, no matter where it led. Being with all three of you, it feels right to me—like a dream come true. But it's scary too because I don't know how any of this will pan out."

"None of us do," Vaughn says softly, reaching out to brush a stray strand of hair from my face. His touch sends a shiver down my spine, igniting an all-too-familiar desire within me.
"

"Exactly," I agree, swallowing hard. "So, we need trust, honesty, and acceptance."

"Even when it's really fucking tough," Zach chimes in, offering a lopsided grin that makes my heart skip a beat. I nod, a genuine smile forming on my lips.

"Especially then," I confirm. "Our bond is stronger than any petty jealousy or fear. We've made magic together on stage, and I believe we can make magic off stage too."

"All right," Vaughn says, nodding. "We'll give it our best shot. For you, and for the sake of the band."

"Promise?" I ask, holding out my pinky finger, a playful grin tugging at the corners of my mouth. They each wrap their own pinkies around mine, sealing our pact with warmth and laughter.

"Promise," they say in unison, their united voices sending a thrill of anticipation coursing through me.

17

FENDER

The sun creeps over the horizon, casting a fiery glow on the walls of my hotel room. A mix of excitement and nervousness churns in the pit of my stomach, threatening to wake me from the half-asleep state I'm lingering in. Today is the day. Our IslandFest performance— the gig that could revive Burn Strategy's career.

I force my eyes open and sit up, rubbing the sleep from them. The weight of today's performance presses down on me, a constant reminder of how important it is for our future. I take a deep breath, trying to quell the anxiety bubbling within me.

Overlaying that is the anxiety that yesterday's lunch discussion provoked.

Did I really agree to be in some sort of man-harem?

What the fuck was I thinking?

"Focus, Fender," I murmur to myself, glancing at the clock on the bedside table. It's still early, but there's no time to waste. I swing my legs over the side of the bed and plant my feet firmly on the floor.

"Countless hours of practice have led us here," I remind myself, thinking back on all the late nights spent perfecting our setlist, the callouses that have formed on my fingertips from strumming my guitar relentlessly. We've poured our hearts and souls into preparing for this moment, and it's finally arrived.

Today's the day we show the world what we're made of.

I stand up, stretching my arms above my head and feeling the familiar ache in my muscles from days of travel and non-stop rehearsals. But it's a small price to pay for the chance to chase our dreams.

As I make my way to the bathroom to splash water on my face, my thoughts drift to Dallas, her captivating stage presence. My throat tightens and I shake my head, trying to dispel the image of her from my thoughts.

Today isn't about any romantic entanglements; it's about giving everything we have to our performance.

I turn on the cold water, cupping my hands and splashing it onto my face. The shock of the icy liquid jolts me back into reality, sharpening my focus.

"Today, it's all about the music," I tell myself again, staring at my reflection in the mirror. "No distractions."

With renewed determination, I dry my face and prepare for the day ahead, knowing that today is the day we'll prove ourselves—not just to the world, but to each other as well. And as I slip on my favorite pair of worn jeans and a black t-shirt, I almost dare to hope that maybe, just maybe, this will be the beginning of something incredible for Burn Strategy.

***

THE SUN BLAZES MERCILESSLY OVERHEAD AS WE GATHER IN THE shade of a palm tree, beads of sweat trickling down our bodies. The salty scent of the sea drifts through the air, mingling with the buzz of anticipation from the crowd already gathered for our show. I scan the faces of my band-mates—Dallas, Vaughn, and Zach—as we huddle together, going over the final details of our performance.

"All right, guys," I say, trying to keep my voice steady despite the nerves gnawing at my insides. "Let's run through the setlist one more time. Make sure we're all on the same page here."

As we discuss the order of songs, I can sense the tension hanging thick among us like a looming storm cloud. It's been impossible to ignore the undercurrent of desire that crackles between Dallas and the rest of the band. Even now, as we try to focus on preparing for the most important show of our lives, it's still there, threatening to derail our focus.

"Are we really opening with 'Velvet Skies'?" Zach questions, breaking into my thoughts. "I thought we were saving that for later in the set."

"Yeah," Dallas chimes in, her green eyes locking onto mine. "I think Velvet Skies' would be perfect for the encore."

Her words send a jolt through me, and I have to force myself to look away from her magnetic gaze. I can feel the weight of her presence, even as she stands several feet away, her lithe figure obscured by the dappled sunlight filtering through the palm fronds above us.

"All right, let's switch it," I agree, clearing my throat. "We'll open with 'First Breaking Point' instead."

"Good call," Vaughn says, nodding his approval. His green eyes flicker briefly to Dallas, and a twinge of jealousy at the unspoken connection between them hits me.

I grit my teeth, reminding myself that now is not the time for petty emotions or distractions. We have worked tirelessly to get here, and I refuse to let anything jeopardize our shot at success—not even my own desire for the fiery woman standing before me.

"Let's nail this performance, guys," I say with as much conviction as I can muster. "We've put in the work, and we know we're ready. Let's show them what Burn Strategy is made of."

As we disperse to make final preparations, I steal one last glance at Dallas, her sun-kissed skin glistening with perspiration. Longing slides through me, fueled by an insatiable hunger for her touch and the burning need to prove ourselves on that stage.

Concentrate, I tell myself. *It's all about the music. No distractions.*

With the sun a fiery, golden orb on the horizon, I make my way backstage to prepare for our performance. The air is thick with anticipation and the scent of saltwater mixed with sweat. My fingers itch to touch my guitar.

"Hey Fender, check this out." Zach holds up a new guitar strap adorned with intricate designs. His dark eyes sparkle with excitement, momentarily casting aside the shadows of doubt that sometimes lurk within them.

"Nice, man," I say, offering him a grin despite the turmoil roiling inside me. I turn my attention to my own guitar, cradled securely in its stand. My hands move deftly along its contours, ensuring everything is in perfect condition for the show.

"Almost time," Vaughn murmurs, his green eyes flicking between each of us as he adjusts the strap of his bass guitar. Despite the outward calm he projects, I can see the faint tremor in his hands—the battle scars of his PTSD that he tries so hard to hide. I clasp his shoulder in silent understanding, and he gives me a small nod of gratitude.

"All right, guys," Dallas pipes up, twirling her drumsticks

effortlessly in her slender fingers. "You ready to rock this island?"

"Damn right," Zach replies, his easygoing smile returning in full force.

"Let's do it," Vaughn adds.

My gaze lingers on Dallas, her blonde hair shimmering like spun gold. It takes every ounce of self-control to keep my hands off her and focus on the task at hand. "We've got this," I say, forcing my voice to remain steady. "We're Burn Strategy, and we're gonna blow them away."

"Here's to the best damn performance of our lives," Dallas says, raising her drumsticks in a salute before making her way to the stage.

"Absolutely," Zach agrees, clapping me on the back as we follow suit.

"Let's make this one count," I say, my heart pounding in my chest—not just for the performance, but for the unspoken desire simmering just beneath the surface between us all. "No distractions, no regrets."

"Agreed," Vaughn murmurs, his gaze meeting mine with a glimmer of understanding.

As the final seconds tick down, we exchange reassuring smiles and nods, a united front in the face of our worries.

"Let's rock, Burn Strategy," I whisper, feeling the comforting weight of my guitar settle against my body.

The roar of the crowd surges around me as I step onto the stage, their anticipation a force that sends adrenaline coursing through my veins. The other two shows were preludes—but here, we're the main event.

My fingers grip the neck of my guitar, feeling the comforting weight of it against my body as I scan the sea of faces before us. This is our moment—our chance to prove ourselves and make a name for Burn Strategy once more.

As the lights dance across the stage, I catch sight of Dallas behind her drum kit, her blonde hair glinting like gold in the vibrant glow. Our eyes lock for an instant, and it's as if time freezes—a brief moment of connection amidst the chaos. In her gaze, I see a reflection of my own desire, my own determination to give everything we've got tonight.

But there's something else there too—an unspoken promise that lingers between us, tantalizing and dangerous.

"Are you ready, IslandFest?!" I shout into the microphone, drawing a deafening cheer from the audience. Their energy courses through me, igniting a fire in my soul that burns brighter with every beat of my heart.

And with a nod to my bandmates, we launch into our opening song.

The music consumes me, wrapping me in its embrace as I lose myself in the intricate dance of chords and melodies. My fingers fly over the fretboard, each note a testament to the countless hours of practice and dedication we've poured into our craft. The lyrics pour from my lips, raw and powerful, carrying the weight of our journey and our dreams.

"Feel the burn, let it take you higher," I sing, my voice soaring above the thunderous rhythm of Dallas' drums. "We're the spark, we'll set your world on fire!"

With every strum of my guitar, every pulse of the bass line, and every crash of the cymbals, we weave a tapestry of sound that captures the essence of who we are. The crowd feeds off our passion, their cheers and applause fueling us to push ourselves even harder.

"Come on, IslandFest!" I call out, my gaze sweeping over the audience as I coax them to join in the chorus. "Let's make this night unforgettable!"

As the music swells around me, I steal glances at Dallas— her lithe form moving with fluid grace behind the drums, her eyes shining with joy.

Tonight, it's about the music, about the bond we share as

a band, and the dreams we've fought so hard to achieve. Tonight, I'll give my all to the performance, pouring my heart and soul into each note and lyric, offering up the raw emotion that lies just beneath the surface.

"Give it up for Burn Strategy!" I cry, raising my guitar high above my head as the last notes fade away. The crowd goes wild, their deafening cheers.

And though I know the tangled web of desire and intrigue that awaits us offstage, in this moment, I am nothing but the music and the fire that burns within.

A bead of sweat drips down my forehead as I strum the opening chords to our next song, my fingers dancing across the strings with practiced ease. The crowd roars in response, their excitement surging through me like a bolt of electricity. For a moment, I glance over at Dallas, her golden hair whipping around her face as she pounds away at her drums with ferocity. Our eyes lock, and for an instant, everything else fades away.

"Are you ready to rock, IslandFest?" I shout into the microphone, my voice cracking just slightly from the intensity of the emotions coursing through me. The crowd cheers back, urging us on, and I grin, my heart swelling with pride.

We launch into another high-energy number.

Dallas' gaze meets mine again, her eyes twinkling with mischief as she mouths the words of the chorus along with me. I smile back, acknowledging the powerful chemistry that crackles between us.

"Sing along with us!" I coax the audience, my voice filled with passion and determination.

As the chorus begins, the crowd belts out the lyrics in unison, their voices ringing out like a beautiful harmony. I steal another glance at Dallas, and she grins at me, her expression filled with warmth and admiration. It's a look that sends shivers down my spine, even as the fire of desire threatens to consume me.

For a moment, I allow myself to bask in the glory of the music and the connection that binds us together on stage. And though I know that the tangled web of desire and intrigue awaits us offstage, tonight, I will let the music transcend any distractions or conflicting emotions. Tonight, I will be nothing but the music and the fire that burns within me.

18

ZACH

The stage lights flash on, momentarily blinding me as I hold my guitar in a firm grip. The familiar weight of it in my hands keeps me grounded, a steadying force amidst the chaos and adrenaline of the performance.

Each strum fills the air with electrifying energy. I immerse myself in the music, feeling it vibrate through every fiber of my being. It's an all-consuming sensation—one that never fails to make me feel alive.

"Are you ready?!" Fender shouts into the microphone, his voice booming across the packed venue. The crowd roars back, and a smile tugs at the corners of my lips.

As we launch into the opening notes of our next song, my eyes inevitably find Dallas. Her blonde hair falls in messy waves around her face as she hammers away at her drum kit, each hit a fierce display of her skill and dedication.

She's a wild storm contained within a small frame,

unyielding and relentless in her pursuit of musical perfection. It's impossible not to be drawn to her.

Our eyes lock at various moments throughout the show, and a thrill runs down my spine each time. It's in these stolen glances that I draw strength from our connection, finding comfort in her presence and the shared passion we have for music.

I wonder if she feels it too, this magnetic pull that threatens to consume us both. But I push those thoughts aside, focusing on maintaining the energy and precision of the performance.

"Give it up for Zach on the rhythm guitar!" Fender calls out, giving me a sly wink as he steps back from the microphone. The spotlight shifts to me, and for a moment, I falter, the weight of the attention bearing down on me like a physical force. But then I see Dallas—her blue eyes shining with encouragement—and my nerves dissipate.

"Show 'em what you got," she mouths, her words drowned out by the cheers of the audience. My heart swells with gratitude and something else—something that feels dangerously close to love.

"All right, let's do this!" I shout back. I launch into a guitar solo, my fingers flying across the frets as if guided by some unseen force. It's in these moments that I feel most alive, when the music takes over and all that exists is the connection between us and our instruments.

We move back into the song, and as it reaches its climax, I steal one last glance at Dallas, my eyes lingering on the curve of her lips and the way her body moves in perfect sync with the rhythm. The desire to reach out and touch her is almost unbearable, but I resist.

"Thank you!" Fender exclaims as the song comes to an end, his voice breathless from the exertion. "You guys rock!"

I nod in agreement, sweat beading on my brow as I catch my breath.

The pounding beat of the drums courses through my veins as the electric energy of the crowd flows over me. Our music has cast its spell, the audience swaying and dancing in raptured unison. Dallas' eyes meet mine again, her lips curving into a wickedly seductive smile that sends shivers down my spine. It's a potent mix, the pull of raw desire and the adrenaline-fueled thrill of the performance.

"Let's kick it up a notch!" Fender shouts from his place at the mic, the anticipation in his voice mirrored by the excited gleam in his eyes. We launch into the next song, the intensity building with each note we play.

Suddenly, amidst the pulsing lights and smoky haze, disaster strikes. A burst of flame erupts from one of the pyrotechnics on stage, the fire spreading rapidly as it feeds off the flammable set pieces. Panic threatens to rise within me, but I force myself to focus, to stay grounded in the moment.

"Vaughn!" I hear Dallas cry out, her voice sharp with alarm. My gaze follows hers, and I see her race toward him, fear etched across her beautiful face. Vaughn stands frozen, his bass guitar forgotten in his hands as the flames lick dangerously close to him, trapped in the grip of his anxiety.

"Everybody, stay calm!" I yell, my voice firm despite the turmoil raging inside me. As much as I want to go to Dallas and protect her, I know that I need to focus on controlling the situation at hand.

"Put out the fires! Keep playing!" I shout to Fender and the others, hoping to maintain some semblance of order. I grab a nearby fire extinguisher and start dousing the flames, my heart pounding in time with the frantic rhythm of the music.

"Zach, help me get Vaughn out of here!" Dallas calls, her

voice tight with urgency. I glance over to see her attempting to pull Vaughn away from the encroaching flames, but he remains rooted in place, his eyes wild and unseeing.

"Vaughn, snap out of it!" I shout, rushing to his side. "We need you, man!"

Fender keeps playing over the chaos, his fingers flying across the keyboard. The music continues, a frenetic backdrop to the crisis unfolding on stage.

19

VAUGHN

The stage lights pulsate in rhythm with the pounding of my heart, intensifying the adrenaline coursing through my veins. As I strum my bass guitar, Fender's voice soars above the music like an eagle riding a thermal. Fender and Zach play their guitars perfectly, and Dallas... God, Dallas. The petite blonde powerhouse behind the drum kit is both our anchor and our spark.

It's going perfectly.

But then...

As the pyrotechnics explode around us, something goes horribly wrong. A blast too close to the stage, a sound that reverberates deep within my chest, sends me spiraling into the past. My heart pounds, panic gripping me as memories of twisted metal and shattered glass from the bus wreck overwhelm me.

"Vaughn!" I barely hear Dallas' voice over the cacophony of noise, but it's enough to pull me back just a little. I take deep breaths, trying to regain control. The music continues without me, my hands frozen above the strings.

"Vaughn, breathe," I hear Dallas say, cutting through the fog in my mind. I glance over at her, and she's left her drums to come to my side. She reaches out to touch my arm, grounding me. It's a small gesture, but it brings me back to reality.

"Come on, man. You've got this," she says, her words laced with encouragement. "We're stronger together, remember?"

I nod, feeling the strength of her conviction, and the warmth of her touch seeps into my skin like a balm to my frayed nerves.

"Vaughn, snap out of it!" Zach shouts as he rushes to his side. "We need you, man!"

The chaos unfolding around me is nearly suffocating, but I refuse to let my fear control me. Crew members are putting the fire out.

Fender's still playing, and I focus on the music, on the band. He starts playing a blistering guitar solo, giving me the perfect opportunity to regain my footing.

"Yeah," I say hoarsely. "I got this."

My fingers find their place on the strings, and I focus on the bassline pulsing through my veins, drowning out the memories threatening to break free. I'm doing this for myself, for Dallas, and for the band.

"Vaughn, you got this," I whisper to myself as I gather my courage and push through my anxiety. The music wraps around me like a protective cocoon, shielding me from my own demons.

I can't let my PTSD define me or hinder our perfor-mance. I won't.

My eyes flicker toward Dallas as she watches me with a mix of concern and support. She gives me a small nod, her gaze never wavering, urging me forward. As soon as she sees that I'm okay, she returns to her drums, her sticks flying across the skins, creating a rhythm that reaches deep into my soul. The band picks up where we left off, the energy sliding through every nerve ending.

"All right! Let's pick it up!" Zach calls out with an encouraging smile, his voice rising above the noise.

I slide my hands along the bass, feeling every note resonate within me. The desire to play, to perform, courses through my veins, blending with my need for Dallas. I focus on the passion we share for our music, the way it connects us, strengthens us, and I let it drive away the dark thoughts clawing at my mind.

"Vaughn, man, you're killing it!" Fender shouts over the music, a grin plastered on his face. His words fill me with pride, further grounding me in the moment.

As the last chords of our song fade away, I glance at Dallas, sweat beading on her forehead as she gives her drums everything she's got. The raw intensity in her rivals the pyrotechnics that should have been illuminating the stage. In this moment, we are one—bound by our love for music and each other.

"Thank you!" I mouth to her over the roar of the crowd, my heart swelling with gratitude and desire. She flashes me a smile, her eyes dancing with mischief and something more— something that makes my pulse race.

With Dallas by my side, I know I'm capable of overcoming anything—even my darkest fears.

The stage lights cast a warm glow over the arena as we continue to play, pushing through the chaos that erupted moments ago. My fingers move across the bass guitar strings, sweat dripping down my temples.

"Vaughn," Zach calls out, his voice steady despite the adrenaline coursing through us all. "Let's switch it up, man!"

I nod and quickly adjust my playing, falling in sync with

Zach's rhythm guitar. Our impromptu change adds a fresh layer to the music, showcasing our adaptability. Fender follows suit, his fingers dancing along the frets of his guitar, weaving intricate solos around our new melody. The crowd roars in approval, their energy fueling our performance.

My gaze flickers to Dallas, who grins back at me from behind her drum kit. She's found her groove again, the beat resonating with my heartbeat as if we are connected on a deeper level.

"All right!" Fender yells, his rebel spirit shining through. "Let's make this a night they'll never forget!"

As we power through our set, improvising and adjusting to the unexpected situation, it's like we're communicating without words—our instruments speaking for us, telling a story of unity and resilience.

"Vaughn, you ready?" Zach asks, his dark brown eyes meeting mine.

"Always," I say, my heart pounding in anticipation. The next song is one of my favorites, a testament to how far we've come as a band and as friends.

"Let's do this!" Dallas chimes in with a wink. I think of how beautiful she looks, the sweat glistening on her skin only enhancing her allure. I swallow hard, forcing myself to focus on the task at hand.

As we launch into the song, my bass guitar becomes an extension of my emotions—every note infused with passion and desire. My eyes remain locked on Dallas, and I can sense her reciprocating my intensity through her vigorous drumming. It's a dance between us, a flirtation that only heightens our connection.

"Vaughn," Fender whispers, "I'm proud of you, man."

As the next song begins, I allow myself to become one with the music. Each note is an outlet for the turmoil churning within me—my PTSD, my desire for Dallas, my love for my brothers in the band. The vibrations from the bass resonate through my chest, driving away the echoes of the past.

The final notes of the song echo through the arena, met by thunderous applause from the crowd.

The crowd roars, a tidal wave of sound crashing over us. My fingers dance across the bass guitar's fretboard, my heart pounding in time with the rhythm. I glance at Dallas, her slender arms wielding the drumsticks like weapons, her fiery red hair shimmering under the stage lights. I think of how beautiful she looks, the sweat glistening on her skin only enhancing her allure. I swallow hard, forcing myself to focus on the task at hand.

"Vaughn," Fender whispers as we near the end of our performance, "I'm proud of you, man."

"Thanks, brother," I say, feeling a surge of gratitude for my bandmates. Together, we've faced this challenge head-on, refusing to let it break us.

"Thank you all so much!" Zach exclaims to the cheering audience. "We couldn't have done it without your support!"

As the applause washes over us, awe and wonder at the power of our shared passion for music overcomes me. It has brought us together, bound us closer than ever before, and allowed us to triumph over adversity. My love for my band-mates—and especially for Dallas—is stronger than ever, and I know that no challenge will ever be insurmountable as long as we face it together.

The crowd's energy surges through the air, a force that fuels our determination to give them the best performance of our lives. As I glance at my bandmates, I see the fire in their eyes, each smile and nod a reminder of our unbreakable bond.

"Let's do this," Fender says, his voice full of conviction, as he strums a powerful chord on his guitar.

"Damn right," Dallas replies, her gaze never leaving mine for a moment, the playful sparkle in her eyes reigniting the desire that simmers beneath the surface. My heart races, not only from the adrenaline of the performance but also from the magnetic pull between us.

We launch into the next song, the music flowing through us like a current, and I'm swept away by the intoxicating combination of passion and unity. Each note we play intertwines with the others, creating a euphoric melody that resonates deep within my soul.

"Come on!" Zach shouts over the roar of the audience, his words punctuated by the rhythmic strumming of his guitar. "You've got this!"

I nod in appreciation, grateful for his unwavering support. As we continue playing, I can feel the growing strength within our bond, forged not just through our love for music but also our shared experiences and struggles.

My fingers glide effortlessly across the strings of my bass guitar, every note a testament to the healing power of music. The weight of my PTSD feels lighter somehow, less suffocating, as if the music has loosened its grip on my heart.

"Look at them," Dallas whispers, her voice barely audible above the din of the crowd. She directs my attention to the sea of faces before us, their expressions filled with awe and admiration.

Our confidence soars as we witness the audience's support for Burn Strategy.

"Thank you!" I shout into the microphone, my voice full of gratitude. "We couldn't do this without you!"

"Guys," I say to the band, my voice barely audible over the roar of the crowd, "we did it."

"Damn right, we did," Dallas replies, her blue eyes sparkling with pride. She slams her drumsticks together, initiating a round of applause just for us, the band.

"Great job, everyone," Zach chimes in, his easygoing smile reaching his eyes. He claps Fender on the shoulder, a gesture of brotherly affection that warms my heart.

I cast a sidelong glance at Dallas, who is radiant with joy. A sudden surge of desire washes over me, making my pulse quicken even more. The way she looks—sweat-soaked and flushed from exertion, her blonde hair wild and tousled—stirs something primal within me.

"Damn right," Fender chimes in, wrapping his arm around my shoulders, that ever-present mischievous glint in his eyes. "What a comeback, huh?"

"Thanks to all of you," I say, my voice choked with emotion. I glance over at Dallas, who's wiping her brow and flashing me a wide, radiant smile.

"Hey, don't forget yourself," she interjects, stepping closer to me. "You held it together out there, and that means everything."

"Here's to Burn Strategy," Fender cheers.

As the cheers and applause rise to an earth-shaking crescendo, I lock eyes with Dallas, Zach, and Fender. There's a rare vulnerability in their gazes, and it hits me deep in my soul. It's as if we've laid ourselves bare on this stage, and now we stand before each other, exposed but triumphant.

20

DALLAS

"Come with me," I say as we finish breaking down from our set and the crew loads our equipment into the van Ezra rented.

My bandmates—my men—all give me slightly confused looks, but they follow my directions.

My heart races as I lead the way to my room, anticipation and nerves causing my hands to shake ever so slightly. The door looms in front of us like a gateway into uncharted territory, and I can feel their eyes on me, watching, waiting.

"Here we are," I say, my voice a bit breathless. I open the door and step inside, turning back to face Vaughn, Zach, and Fender. "Please, come in."

They enter cautiously, and I notice the uncertainty in their gazes. It's mirrored in my own feelings, but I'm determined to make them feel welcome.

"Make yourselves comfortable," I tell them, gesturing to the various seating options scattered around the room. They do as I suggest, finding spots on chairs and the edge of the bed, their bodies tense with the weight of what they assume we're about to discuss.

Vaughn, his dark hair tousled and eyes intense, leans against the wall with a small smile playing on his lips. Zach stands by the window, arms crossed over his chest, his green eyes sparkling with curiosity. Fender, his muscular frame filling the doorway, simply nods at my words.

I move around the room, lighting candles and turning on soft music. Then I turn to face them.

"Thanks for coming," I begin, struggling to find the right words. "I thought it was important for us to talk, you know, about...us."

"Us?" Fender questions, his gaze meeting mine.

"Yeah, us," I confirm, my heart pounding in my chest. "Look, I know this is unconventional and maybe even a little crazy, but I've been thinking a lot about our connections lately, both individually and as a group."

Vaughn shifts uncomfortably, his green eyes filled with concern. "Dallas, are you sure this is something you want to dive into?"

I nod, resolute. "Yes, I am. I can't ignore how I feel anymore. And I don't think you guys can either."

Zach clears his throat, his dark eyes searching mine. "So, what exactly are you saying?"

Taking a deep breath, I decide to let it all out. "What I'm saying is that I love each of you. And not just as friends or bandmates. I'm in love with you, Fender, Vaughn, and Zach."

There's a moment of stunned silence before Fender speaks up again. "Do you really mean that?"

"Yes," I say firmly, my gaze unwavering. "I want to be with all of you. However that looks, whatever it means for the band."

"Are you certain?" Vaughn asks, his voice filled with

doubt. "A polyamorous relationship could cause problems within the band. It's risky."

"Everything about us is risky," I counter. "We're rock stars, living on the edge. And besides," I add, meeting each of their eyes in turn, "our connection is special. It's unique. And it's worth fighting for."

"Even if it causes complications?" Zach questions.

"Even then," I say, my conviction unwavering. "Because at the end of the day, we're stronger together than we are apart."

As they exchange glances, I can see the wheels turning in their minds, weighing the risks against the potential rewards. Their hesitance is palpable, but so is my desire for them. And so, I take one final leap, baring myself to them completely.

"Look," I say, my words coming out almost as a whisper. "I want you all. Every single one of you, in every way possible."

And with that, the room goes silent, as heavy with anticipation as it is with desire. Only time will tell if this gamble pays off, but as I stand before the three men who hold my heart, I know one thing for certain: I wouldn't trade this moment for anything in the world.

"Darlin', we all feel the same way about you," Vaughn drawls, his voice low and soothing like molasses.

"Absolutely," Zach chimes in, his gaze never leaving mine. "You're the heartbeat of this band."

Fender, ever the man of few words, just inclines his head in agreement.

My face flushes with warmth at their words, and I take a deep breath to steady myself.

The candlelight casts shadows on the walls, flickering like the emotions swirling within me. The soft music weaves itself into the room, creating a cocoon of intimacy. I turn my gaze to Vaughn, my fingers absentmindedly twirling a strand of my blonde hair.

"Vaughn," I begin, my voice barely above a whisper. "Your talent for writing songs is unmatched. You have this incredible ability to mix raw emotion with beautiful melodies."

A hint of a smile tugs at the corners of his lips, and his green eyes seem to glow. He opens his mouth to speak, but I raise a hand to stop him. I need to say this before I lose my nerve.

"Zach," I continue, turning to face him. His dark hair falls over one eye, but the intensity of his gaze is still evident. "You're not just an amazing guitarist, but also the glue that holds us together when things get tough. Your quiet strength and unwavering dedication to the band inspires us all."

His cheeks flush slightly, and he nods his head, a look of appreciation etched across his face.

Lastly, I turn to Fender. Despite his stoic exterior, I know there's a fierce passion that burns within him. "Fender, you add depth and soul to our music. There's an energy about you that's magnetic, drawing people in even if they don't quite understand why. You bring a sense of balance to the chaos, and I'm grateful to have you by my side."

Fender doesn't respond verbally, but the slight lift of his brow lets me know that my words have reached him.

My eyes flicker between Vaughn, Zach, and Fender, each of their faces reflecting their own emotions. It feels like time has stopped, leaving us suspended in this intimate bubble where the outside world doesn't exist—only the space between us and the unspoken feelings we've carried for so long.

"Thank you," I whisper once more, the words heavy with meaning. "For everything."

And as the soft music continues to play, our bond deepens, ready to face whatever challenges lie ahead.

The flickering candlelight casts dancing shadows on the

walls of my small bedroom, creating an intimate atmosphere that seems to mirror the emotions swirling within me.

Fender finally breaks his silence, his eyes locked on mine with an intensity that makes my stomach flutter. "I'm not gonna lie. I'm scared. Not just for the band, but for you. A relationship like this... it could hurt you, and I never want to see you in pain." His words are laced with a raw vulnerability that sends a shiver down my spine.

"Can we agree to take this one step at a time?" I suggest, my voice barely louder than a whisper. "We don't have to figure everything out right now. But let's not shy away from exploring these feelings, either. We owe it to ourselves, and to each other, to see where this might lead."

The room is heavy with tension, but as I hold their gazes, I know that we're all willing to try.

A moment of silence follows, the tension thickening in the air. Then, slowly, they each nod in agreement, their expressions filled with hope. My heart swells with love for these extraordinary men who have changed my life, and I know that I'll do whatever it takes to make this work.

I exhale, my body trembling with anticipation as I stand up and walk toward the center of the room. Their eyes follow me, filled with a mixture of desire and uncertainty. I can feel the intensity of their gazes like a physical touch.

"I want you all—Fender, Vaughn, and Zach." As if to punctuate my words, I reach behind me and slowly unzip my dress, allowing the silky fabric to slide down my body, pooling at my feet. The air kisses my skin, and I shiver with anticipation.

"Are you sure about this?" Vaughn asks. I can see the love in his eyes, as well as the fear of what this might mean for our band and our future.

"More than anything," I say, my words filled with conviction. "I've never been more sure of anything in my life."

21

I stand in the center of the hotel room, the floor-to-ceiling windows revealing an enchanting view of the island. The sound of crashing waves and rustling palm trees outside does little to ease my pounding heart. Naked and vulnerable, I swallow, my gaze darting between Vaughn, Zach, and Fender. My pulse races with excitement and uncertainty. What if they reject me? Can we go back to just being a band after this?

Fender continues leaning against the door, his arms crossed over his chest, studying me intently. He's always been the leader of our group, pushing boundaries and challenging norms, but even he seems hesitant now. I search his gaze for any hint of reluctance or doubt.

"More than anything, huh?" he finally says, his voice low and rough. His rebellious spirit ignites mine, and I nod.

Without another word, Fender pushes off from the door and crosses the room in three long strides. He grabs my waist, pulling me against his hard body, and kisses me roughly. His lips are demanding, possessive—a firestorm of passion that leaves no room for doubt or hesitation. I moan into his mouth, my hands gripping his muscular shoulders.

"God, you're so beautiful," he murmurs, breaking the kiss for a moment to look me in the eye. "I've wanted this since the moment I saw you."

I shudder at his confession, feeling desired and cherished in a way I never thought possible.

Fender's strong arms lift me off the ground effortlessly, and I wrap my legs around his waist as he carries me to the bed. He lays me down, and a shiver runs down my spine as the cool sheets contact my heated skin.

"Are you okay?" Fender asks, stretching out next to me.

"More than okay," I assure him, pulling him down for another searing kiss.

As we break apart again, Vaughn rises from his chair, having remained silent during the initial exchange between Fender and me. His green eyes lock onto mine, and I can see the quiet strength behind them as he moves toward the bed.

"Can I...?" Vaughn's voice is hesitant, but his gaze remains steady.

"Please," I breathe.

He crawls onto the bed, settling himself between my thighs. His fingers trail over my inner thighs, teasingly light, making me squirm in anticipation. The moment his lips touch my sensitive flesh, a moan escapes my throat. My back arches involuntarily, pushing myself closer to Vaughn's eager mouth.

"Vaughn," I gasp, my hands finding purchase in his sandy brown hair, urging him on. My mind races, trying to process the overwhelming sensations coursing through my body.

"Is this what you want?" Fender whispers in my ear, his breath hot against my skin. "Tell us what you need."

"More," I manage to choke out, desperate for the pleasure that Fender, Vaughn, and Zach can provide.

"Remember, you asked for this," Fender says with a wicked grin.

As Vaughn's talented mouth continues to work its magic, I find it increasingly difficult to focus on anything else. My thoughts are consumed by the intense desire that pulses through me, heightened by the knowledge that these three incredible men are here to share this experience with me.

"God, you're amazing," I tell Vaughn, my voice barely audible above the sound of my own panting.

"Anything for you," he murmurs against my skin before returning his full attention to the task at hand.

In that moment, I realize just how much I am loved and desired by these men.

The blaze inside me burns, my body arching in response to the sensations that flood my senses. Fender's lips find mine, stealing my breath as he kisses me deeply, our tongues dancing in a passionate duel. I moan into his mouth again, unable to contain the pleasure that threatens to consume me.

"Let it out, baby," Fender urges between heated kisses, his words low and seductive.

As if on cue, Zach moves closer, his strong hands gently cupping my breasts as he begins to tease and play with my sensitive nipples. A shiver runs down my spine, heightened by the salty sea air that fills the room.

"Beautiful," Zach murmurs, his warm breath tickling my skin before his lips descend onto one nipple, sucking and nipping at it while his fingers continue their expert ministrations on the other.

"Zach... yes..." I whimper, my voice barely above a whisper. The room spins around me, but the only thing that matters is the electrifying touch of these three men.

"Enjoying yourself?" Fender asks, his eyes gleaming with mischief.

"More than you can imagine," I gasp out.

"Good," Fender growls, his lips brushing against mine once more, as if he can't bear to be apart from me for even a second. "We're just getting started."

"Promise?" I ask, grinning despite the haze of pleasure that clouds my thoughts.

"Absolutely," Vaughn chimes in, his voice muffled against my inner thigh. As if to punctuate his statement, he redoubles his efforts, sending shockwaves of ecstasy through my body.

As Fender's mouth continues to devour mine, Vaughn's tongue works its magic between my legs, and Zach teases and sucks on my breasts, I know deep down that I've found something truly rare and precious in these three men. I am their muse, their lover, their heartbeat—and they are mine. Together, we are unstoppable, a force of nature as powerful and wild as the rolling waves that crash against the island's shores.

And in this moment, lost in the whirlwind of passion and desire that surrounds us, I think that maybe, just maybe, this is where I was always meant to be.

A tidal wave of pleasure surges through me, uncontrollable and wild. The combined sensations of Fender's possessive kiss, Vaughn's skilled tongue, and Zach's teasing lips on my breasts send me hurtling toward an explosive climax. Every nerve in my body pulses with electric ecstasy as I cry out their names.

The intensity of my orgasm leaves me breathless and vulnerable, my limbs trembling from the aftershocks. Fender finally breaks our feverish kiss, his blue eyes dark with desire as they lock onto mine. "You're incredible," he whispers, his voice rough.

"Thank you," I manage to gasp, still reeling from the unbelievable high they've just given me. But something tells me we're far from done, and I can't help the thrill that courses through me at the thought.

Fender stands up and steps back, his gaze never leaving mine as he begins to undress. Heat pools in my core as I watch the tantalizing reveal of his toned muscles and tattoos. Vaughn and Zach follow suit, stripping down with an unhurried grace that only serves to heighten my craving for them.

My eyes dart between the three of them, taking in every inch of their naked glory, and I'm struck with the overwhelming reality of what's about to happen. A mixture of excitement, lust, and the slightest hint of trepidation floods through me, but it's the burning desire for these men that ultimately wins out.

"God, you're all so..." I trail off, the words caught in my throat as I attempt to articulate the sheer magnitude of my feelings. How do you put into words the experience of having your wildest dreams come to life before your very eyes?

"Ready for you," Zach supplies, stepping closer and cupping my face in his strong hands.

"Let us take care of you," Vaughn murmurs from behind me, his fingers tracing delicate patterns across my shoulder. The intimate touch sends shivers down my spine, a testament to just how well he knows my body after only a short time.

"Trust us," Fender adds, his voice commanding. And despite the whirlwind of emotions swirling within me, I realize that's exactly what I want—to trust them with my heart, my body, and my soul.

"Always," I breathe, surrendering myself completely to the passion that awaits.

Fender, a pillar of strength and control, lies down on the

bed, his gaze never leaving mine. He pulls me atop him, and I can feel the heat radiating from our skin as it connects.

"Are you ready for this?" he asks.

"Oh, yes, yes please," I say, my voice shaking with excitement and nerves. His lips curl into a smile before he slowly pulls me toward him, sliding me down on his cock until he fills me completely. The sensation is overwhelming, every nerve ending in my body igniting as he stretches me, making me feel more alive than ever.

"Ah, Fender…" My head drops back as I moan his name, reveling in the connection we share. It's then that I feel Zach lean over from behind me, his warm breath grazing my neck as he whispers, "You're so beautiful like this."

Before I can respond, he captures my lips in a searing kiss, his tongue dancing with mine as Fender continues to move inside me. My body feels like an inferno.

"Vaughn…" I gasp between kisses, needing to feel him too, to be surrounded by their love and devotion. I hear a soft chuckle, and Vaughn's hand wraps around my waist, pulling me closer.

"Patience, love," he murmurs, his thumb tracing lazy circles around my navel. "We have all night."

"Please," I beg, desperate for the complete union of our bodies, minds, and souls.

As Fender thrusts into me, Zach's lips never leaving mine, and Vaughn's touch setting my skin ablaze, I realize that this is more than just a single night of passion.

"Are you okay?" Fender asks, concern etched across his handsome face as he slows his movements.

"Never been better," I assure him, my eyes locked with his. "I love you."

"I love you too," he replies, and in that instant, I know that this is it—our souls have finally found their way home.

And yet, he doesn't pick up the pace.

I figure out why moments later.

"Trust me?" Zach whispers into my ear as his strong hands rest on my hips. I nod, leaning forward slightly to give him better access. The sensation of Fender's cock inside my pussy already has me trembling with need, but the thought of Zach joining us only intensifies the desire coursing through my veins.

"Okay," I breathe out, closing my eyes and focusing on the connection between our bodies. The head of Zach's cock presses against my ass, and I force myself to relax, trusting in his love for me.

"Easy now," he murmurs, slowly pushing himself inside me. The initial discomfort is quickly overshadowed by the thrill of being filled by two men. Inch by inch, Zach works his way into me until I can feel his pelvis pressed against my backside.

"Are you okay?" Fender asks, his movements still paused.

"Yes," I gasp, letting out a shaky laugh. "I'm more than okay."

"Good," Zach says softly, planting a kiss on my shoulder. "We're here for you."

As if in sync, Fender and Zach begin moving inside me— their dual rhythm sending waves of pleasure coursing through my body. My fingers grip the bedsheets, overwhelmed by the sheer intensity of it all.

"God, I love you both so much," I moan, my voice barely audible over the pounding of my heart.

"We love you too," Fender replies, his voice strained with passion.

"Always," Zach adds, his breath hot against my skin.

The sensation of Fender and Zach moving inside me is a sensory overload, nearly blinding in its intensity. My body quivers with each thrust, caught between pleasure and the edge of something transcendent. It's a heady mix—the heat of their bodies, the intoxicating scent of sweat and arousal, the sound of our ragged breaths mingling in the air.

"God, you're so beautiful like this," Fender growls, his fingers gripping my hips with bruising strength.

"Thank you," I whisper, my voice trembling with emotion. And it's true—I feel powerful and vulnerable all at once, a goddess brought to life by their worshipful touch.

My eyes flutter open, and I'm met with the sight of Vaughn standing beside the bed. He's naked, his lean and muscular body illuminated by the flickering candlelight. His cock is hard and proud, and I can see the evidence of his desire for me glistening at the tip.

"Vaughn" I breathe, my heart swelling with love for him. "Please… I need you."

"Are you sure?" he asks, hesitating despite the clear hunger in his eyes. Even now, with the weight of his own desires bearing down on him, he's still thinking of me and my well-being.

"Absolutely," I assure him, reaching out a hand to beckon him closer. "I want to taste you."

Vaughn steps forward until he's within reach. I take hold of his cock, feeling the warmth and hardness of him against my palm.

"Trust me" I plead, my gaze locked on his. "I need this—we all do."

"Okay" he whispers, giving in to the magnetic pull that's been tugging at us since the moment we met. With trembling hands, I guide him toward my mouth, parting my lips in anticipation.

The instant I take him in, it's as if a missing piece of our puzzle finally falls into place. The taste of him—salty and sweet—only adds to the cocktail of sensations coursing through me, and I moan around him.

"God, Dallas," Vaughn gasps, his fingers threading through my hair as I take him deeper.

With Vaughn's cock in my mouth and the synchronized thrusts of Fender and Zach filling me completely, I'm consumed by pleasure.

"Fuck, Dallas... you feel so incredible," Fender growls, his eyes locked on mine as he pushes deeper inside me. His gaze is so intense, it feels like he can see straight into my soul.

"Tell us what you need, baby," Zach urges softly, his breath hot against my ear as he continues to move in unison with Fender. "We're here for you."

Vaughn pulls out of my mouth long enough to allow me to speak.

"More..." I moan, my voice barely audible between the frenzied pants and gasps that escape my lips. "I need more of all of you."

Zach grins, a wicked glint in his dark brown eyes. He increases his pace, driving his cock even harder into my ass while Fender matches his rhythm. Meanwhile, Vaughn grips my hair, guiding my head as I suck him deeper.

I cry out around Vaughn as the first orgasm hits, a powerful wave of ecstasy that ripples through my body with such force that I nearly lose my grip on Vaughn. But he steadies me, his green eyes filled with concern and tenderness.

"Are you okay?" he asks, his voice strained from the effort of holding back his own release.

I nod fervently, my eyes tearing up from the intensity of the moment.

The three of them redouble their efforts, each man letting out a low growl or groan that only serves to heighten my arousal. My body trembles uncontrollably, wave after wave of shuddering orgasms washing over me as they continue to fuck me in perfect harmony.

I pull my mouth away from Vaughn long enough to speak again. "Come for me," I beg, desperate to share in their pleasure. "Come inside me, all of you."

And, as if on cue, Fender, Vaughn, and Zach surrender to the moment, each man releasing deep within me one by one —first Fender, then Zach, and finally Vaughn, his warm seed filling my mouth as I swallow eagerly. It's a beautiful, intimate communion.

And I want it to happen again and again.

"God, I love you all so much," I pant, tears streaming down my cheeks. "I never knew it could be like this."

"Neither did we," Fender admits, his blue eyes shining with unshed tears. "But now that we've found you, we're never letting go."

"Me too," Zach and Vaughn echo in unison, their voices filled with raw emotion.

The scent of sweat and sex hangs heavy in the air as we lay tangled together, limbs intertwined and hearts beating as one. The flickering candlelight casts a warm glow on Fender's chiseled features, Vaughn's dark curls, and Zach's piercing gaze—three ruggedly handsome faces that I've come to adore more than anything.

And in that moment, enveloped by the embrace of these three incredible men, I know that I've found something truly precious: a love that transcends convention, defies boundaries, and ignites my very soul.

"Wow," Fender breathes, his fingers tracing lazy circles on my thigh. "That was... something else."

"Something incredible," Vaughn adds, a contented smile playing at the corners of his lips. "I never thought I'd feel this way about anyone, let alone a woman I'm sharing with two other guys."

"Same here," Zach admits, his strong hand gently stroking my hair. "But it feels right, you know?"

"Guys," I murmur, my voice choked with feeling. "I don't know what the future holds for us, but I want you to know that I'm all in. No matter what."

"Me too," Fender vows, his steely resolve sending shivers down my spine. "We're in this together, now and always."

"Damn straight," Zach agrees, his fiery passion igniting something deep within me.

"Here's to the four of us," Vaughn declares, raising an imaginary glass in toast. "May our love always burn as brightly as it does tonight."

"Here's to us," we echo in unison, our voices filled with hope and promise.

But for now, wrapped in the arms of my lovers, my friends, and my bandmates, I am content to simply bask in the afterglow of our connection, knowing that whatever challenges life throws our way, we'll face them together.

EPILOGUE

EZRA, ONE MONTH LATER

The sun sets low on the Denver skyline as I stand by the window of my office, nursing a glass of whiskey.

It's been a whirlwind few months for all of us since IslandFest, and as I take in the breathtaking view, I think back to the rollercoaster journey Burn Strategy has endured, from the harrowing loss of their drummer that shook them to their core, to the miraculous moment when Dallas joined their ranks and breathed new life into the band.

I'm so glad I got to see them perform. I'd almost missed my last-minute flight, but I'll never forget the electric energy that coursed through the crowd at IslandFest when they took the stage—it was like witnessing a phoenix rising from the ashes.

"Hey, Ezra, you got a minute?" Fender's voice interrupts my thoughts. He leans against the doorframe with his arms crossed, his gaze searching mine. His grief and guilt still flicker in those eyes, but there's a newfound light in him, too.

149

"Of course," I say, setting my glass down and gesturing for him to enter. "What's on your mind?"

"Thought you might want to see this." He hands me a stack of magazine clippings, the pages filled with glowing reviews and interviews about their triumphant performance at IslandFest. I smile as I scan the headlines, each one praising Burn Strategy's impressive resurgence.

I've read most of these already, but there are a few in the pile that I haven't seen before.

"These are amazing," I say, genuinely impressed by the outpouring of support from fans and critics alike.

"Right?" Fender grins, clearly proud of what they've accomplished. "Seems like everyone's finally starting to see what we're capable of."

"More than that, they're recognizing the impact you've made on the music scene." My chest swells with pride as I hand the clippings back to him. "You've got some real momentum now, and we can't afford to waste it."

Fender nods in agreement, his expression growing serious. "That's why we need your guidance more than ever."

"Hey, that's what I'm here for," I say, clapping him on the shoulder. "We'll make sure Burn Strategy reaches its full potential."

As he leaves my office, a twinge of anxiety mixes with my excitement. The band's meteoric rise has been nothing short of miraculous, and I'm determined to ensure their continued success. But as I look out over the Denver skyline once more, I worry about the complexities that come with managing a group of talented, passionate individuals, each with their own unique set of strengths, weaknesses, and desires.

THE SUN CASTS LONG SHADOWS ACROSS THE FLOOR OF THEIR rehearsal space, and I watch as Burn Strategy sets up their gear. They're glowing with the energy of their recent success. Fender is meticulously tuning his guitar, his blue eyes focused and determined, while Zach plugs in his own guitar with an easy smile on his face. Vaughn picks up his bass and starts playing a familiar riff. Meanwhile, Dallas jokes around as she adjusts her drum kit, her laughter bright and infectious.

"All right, guys," I begin, clapping my hands together to get their attention. "I know you're still riding high from IslandFest, but we need to discuss our next steps. With all the buzz surrounding Burn Strategy, we have a golden chance to capitalize on this momentum."

As I speak, I notice how physically close they all seem to be. Fender's hand brushes against Zach's shoulder, lingering for a moment before he pulls away. Dallas leans into Vaughn, whispering something in his ear that makes him chuckle softly. It's as if there's an invisible thread drawing them all together.

"Hey, what's going on with you guys?" I ask, curious about the shift in their dynamic. "You all seem... closer than usual."

They exchange glances, and for a moment, no one speaks. Then Fender clears his throat, looking me squarely in the eye. "We've been through a lot together," he says, his voice steady yet laced with an unspoken emotion. "It's brought us closer, made us realize how much we care about each other, both as bandmates and as friends."

"Sure." I nod. They've experienced incredible triumphs and crushing losses, and it's only natural for their relationships to evolve as a result. But as their manager, I worry about the potential complications that could arise from this newfound closeness.

"Listen," I say, trying to keep my tone light even as my

concern grows. "I'm glad you guys are so supportive of each other. It's part of what makes Burn Strategy special. But remember, we have a unique opportunity right now, and we need to stay focused on our goals."

Fender nods, his expression serious. "We know. We wouldn't let anything get in the way of our success."

"Good," I say, relieved by his reassurance. "Now, let's talk about our next steps. I've been working on securing some high-profile gigs and festival appearances for us, and there's interest from several record labels in signing a new deal with Burn Strategy."

As we dive into our discussion, hashing out plans and strategies for the future, I can't shake the uneasiness that lingers at the back of my mind. The band's newfound intimacy is both heartwarming and worrisome, and I silently hope that it won't prove to be a distraction or an obstacle in our path to even greater success.

But the band seems weirdly close. They exchange affectionate touches and share inside jokes, their laughter filling the room. Dallas seems to be at the center of it all, her eyes sparkling with mischief as she flits from one man to another.

I try to push aside the nagging feeling that something is going on here that I'm not entirely privy to, but I can't.

"All right, guys," I finally say. "Seriously—what's going on? This isn't just getting closer as friends."

Dallas exchanges glances with the other band members, and for a moment, there's an unspoken understanding that passes between them. Then, she takes a deep breath and says, "I'm dating all the guys in the band."

"Wait, seriously?" The words slip out before I can stop myself, and my jaw drops open in shock. As much as I've noticed the increased camaraderie between them, I never would have guessed that it had developed into something romantic.

Fuck, that's why I chose her—Dallas has a well-documented aversion to commitment.

At least, she did.

"Yep," Dallas confirms, her voice steady even as her cheeks flush slightly pink. "It's a little unconventional, sure, but it's working for us. And don't worry—we've talked about it, and we're all committed to keeping our personal lives separate from our professional ones."

"All right then," I say slowly, still trying to process this unexpected revelation. Part of me wants to ask more questions—to understand how this happened, and what it means for the future of Burn Strategy.

But ultimately, I remind myself that their personal lives are just that—personal. My job is to guide them as a band, not meddle in their romantic affairs.

"Thanks for telling me," I tell her, forcing a smile onto my face. "As long as you're all happy and able to focus on your music, that's what matters. Now, let's get back to discussing our next steps as a band."

As we dive back into our conversation, I find myself grappling with a strange mix of emotions—surprise at their unorthodox relationship, worry about the potential complications it could cause, and yes, maybe even the tiniest twinge of jealousy.

———

THE LOS ANGELES SUN SHINES BRIGHTLY OUTSIDE THE window as I step into the sleek, modern office of the record label executive. The walls are adorned with platinum records and signed guitars—a testament to the power this company holds within the music industry.

"Mr. Sinclair, thank you for meeting with me," I say, extending my hand firmly. He's a middle-aged man with salt-

and-pepper hair, dressed in an impeccably tailored suit. His eyes are sharp, but there's a genuine warmth in his smile as he shakes my hand.

"Please, call me Joseph," he replies, gesturing for me to take a seat opposite him. "I've been looking forward to discussing Burn Strategy's future with you."

As we engage in small talk about the band's recent success at IslandFest, I feel a surge of pride. Despite the loss of their original drummer and the emotional scars it left behind, they've come back stronger than ever.

But now, with the knowledge of their unconventional romantic arrangement, I'm more determined than ever to protect their professional growth.

"Well, Joseph, given the overwhelming response from fans and critics alike, I think it's time for a new recording contract that reflects Burn Strategy's renewed status in the music industry," I say, laying out my proposal on the polished wood table between us. "Their talent is undeniable, and I believe they have the potential to reach even greater heights."

He nods thoughtfully, scanning the documents I've provided. "I agree. The band has shown tremendous resilience and growth. We're prepared to offer them a more lucrative deal, ensuring they have the resources needed to continue their upward trajectory."

"Thank you," I say, relief washing over me. Securing this contract will not only validate their hard work, but also reaffirm my role in their lives—as their manager and friend.

"There's one more thing I need to discuss with you," I say, my voice steady despite the unease churning in my stomach. "The band members have recently entered into a unique romantic arrangement with one another. It's important that this doesn't hinder their professional growth."

He raises an eyebrow, clearly taken aback. But to his credit, he quickly composes himself and leans back in his chair, considering my words. "As long as their personal lives don't interfere with their music and they continue to deliver outstanding performances, I don't see why it should be an issue."

"Exactly," I agree, feeling another twinge of jealousy that I quickly push aside. After all, what matters most is the success and happiness of Burn Strategy—both personally and professionally. "I just wanted to make sure we're on the same page."

"Absolutely," Joseph confirms, extending his hand once more. As our handshake seals the deal, I vow to myself that I'll do everything in my power to ensure the complexities of their odd polyamorous romance won't stand in the way of Burn Strategy's bright future.

———

TWO DAYS LATER, I GATHER EVERYONE TOGETHER AT MY favorite meeting place outside my office—a cozy, dimly lit coffeehouse in the heart of Denver. The scent of freshly brewed coffee and pastry dough fills my senses, while Burn Strategy's members sit before me: Fender, Zach, Vaughn, and Dallas.

"Guys," I begin. "First and foremost, congratulations on your incredible success at IslandFest. We've just signed a new recording contract that reflects your renewed status in the music industry."

"Seriously?" Dallas exclaims.

"Absolutely," I confirm, holding up the contract for all to see.

"Fuck yeah, man! That's amazing!" Fender grins, his eyes lighting up.

"However," I continue, my tone turning serious, "we need to discuss managing your public image and maintaining a balance between your personal lives and your professional careers."

"Of course," Vaughn says, his green eyes locked on mine, understanding the gravity of the situation.

"Given your... unique romantic arrangement," I say, trying to keep my voice steady, "it's crucial that we handle this aspect of your lives carefully. We don't want it to overshadow your music or hinder your careers."

"Totally get it," Zach agrees, his dark brown eyes flicking between each member of the group, who all nod their agreement, too.

"Good," I nod, relieved by their understanding. "Now, onto more exciting news." I pause for dramatic effect, unable to contain the grin spreading across my face. "I've organized a party tonight to celebrate your achievements. It will be held at Club Verve"—one of Denver's hottest spots.

"Seriously?" Dallas glances around at the other band members. Her three boyfriends, I think with stunned surprise, and not for the first time.

"Thanks," Fender says, clapping me on the back. "We appreciate everything you've done for us."

"Of course. Let's toast to your success and then get ready to party tonight!" I say, raising my coffee cup in the air.

"Cheers!" we all shout in unison, clinking our cups together. The rich aroma of coffee fills my nostrils as I take a sip, savoring the moment and silently vowing to guide Burn Strategy down the path to even greater heights.

WE HAVE ANOTHER PARTY THE NIGHT THEIR FIRST SINGLE drops. It's in full swing, and I stand on the balcony of Club Verve, whiskey in hand, looking down at the sea of people dancing and mingling below. The pulsating beat of Burn

Strategy's single, "Our Secrets," thumps through the speakers, and the crowd is electrified by the music.

"Hey, Ezra," Dallas says, sidling up next to me with a drink in hand. She leans against the railing, her laughter ringing out like the chime of delicate bells. "Quite a party you threw for us. Thanks!"

"Anything for you guys," I say with a genuine smile, my chest swelling with pride. "You've earned it."

"Damn right we have," she agrees, raising her glass in a toast. We clink our glasses together, the sound crisp and clear amidst the noise of the party.

"You know," I say, taking a deep breath as I look at the band members enjoying themselves below, "it's been incredible watching you all grow as musicians and as people. And I think that part of your recent success has something to do with the... unique dynamic you share with the guys."

Dallas laughs softly, her eyes twinkling. "You mean the fact that I'm fucking all of them? Yeah, maybe." She takes a sip of her drink, her gaze drifting to where Fender, Zach, and Vaughn are sharing a private joke.

I watch them too, and I see the way they support and protect one another. They lean into each other, laughing and whispering in a tight circle; their connection is undeniable.

It's not my place to judge or interfere, I remind myself. My job is to manage and promote the band—and they're happier and more successful than ever.

"Whatever works, right?" I say, forcing a smile. "As long as the band keeps making great music, I'm happy."

"Thank you," Dallas says. "We couldn't have done it without you."

"Hey, that's what I'm here for," I say. "And I can't wait to see what the future holds for Burn Strategy."

"Me too." Dallas grins, her eyes full of excitement and anticipation.

I glance back at the party as Dallas flits away to join her men. I'm proud of the band. Their resilience and talent have propelled them to new heights in their musical careers, and I acknowledge that their success is due in part to the men's relationship with Dallas.

"Here's to the future," I murmur to myself, raising my glass before taking a sip of the amber liquid. It burns going down, much like the challenges we'll face together. But in the end, I know Burn Strategy is destined to leave an indelible mark on the world of music.

And I, for one, wouldn't miss it for anything.

ABOUT THE AUTHORS

USA Today, *Wall Street Journal*, and *New York Times* bestselling author **Margo Bond Collins** is a former college English professor who, tired of explaining the difference between "hanged" and "hung," turned to writing romance novels instead. Sometimes her heroines kill monsters, sometimes they kiss aliens. But they always aim for the heart.

Want to hang out with the author, win book prizes, see the cool covers first, and support Margo's books on social media? Join The Vampirarchy, Margo's street team on Facebook!

USA Today bestselling author **London Kingsley** writes steamy contemporary romance with a dark twist. She is the co-author of the King of Clubs series with Margo Bond Collins and the co-author of the Sons of Gods MC series with Elizabeth Knox, beginning with Erupt.

Ingram Content Group UK Ltd.
Milton Keynes UK
UKHW020836210723
425555UK00014B/486